family
genus
species

kevin allardice

Outpost19 | San Francisco
outpost19.com

Allardice, Kevin
        Family, Genus, Species/ Kevin Allardice
        ISBN 9781944853204 (pbk)

Library of Congress Control Number: 2016918546

OUTPOST19

ORIGINAL
PROVOCATIVE
READING

Also by
Kevin Allardice

Any Resemblance to Actual Persons

family
genus
species

One.

Vee just wants to know where to put the present. She's gripping it, two-handedly, thumbs flicking the curled-up corners of tape. She's holding it at a distance like a bomb, or maybe just something smelly.

She wants to set it down on what she expected to be a mountain of other gifts—a mountain so big it would be going avalanchey with abundance—all those presents in glossy wrapping paper of pastels and neons: bright beribboned things, she imagined.

The wrapping paper on the gift she's brought, on the other hand, is not the garish birthday-splash kind of wrapping paper. The guy at the toy store who wrapped it for her, he gave her the option of those papers—one with rubbery but flat characters she could almost recognize from cartoons Vlad watches when he's stoned—but she opted for a paper with tasteful paisley, figured Charlie would appreciate the amoeba-like patterns. After all, Vee's sister, Pam, Charlie's mother, told her Charlie is interested in science. "Oh," Vee said, "he's just like me!" And Pam scoffed, said, "Let's hope not," then said Charlie will surely major in one of the STEM fields one day at Penn or maybe Brown (Pam and Geoff have already ruled out the top tier Ivies after Charlie's pre-K tests).

So Vee just wants to know where to set the gift down, but, wandering her sister's backyard—a sprawling urban farm whose layout of garden beds seems designed to frustrate—she finds no pile of presents.

None at all.

She sees only loose scrambles of small children, from

diaper-age to first grade, skittering through the yard. Screaming or squealing, she can't be sure.

She finds a man standing with a beer at an intersection of kale, arugula, and what appears to be either a cabbage plant or a prop from *Little Shop of Horrors*. The man is wearing a backpack, a backpack made to look dude-friendly but is clearly a diaper bag, its straps buckled over a belly he's trying to hold in muscular poise.

"Scuse me," she says, "where does this go?" She holds up the present.

He looks her over. She's suddenly aware of her army surplus jacket, its baggy obscuring of her body. He returns his gaze to the fruit trees in the distance. "I dunno. My wife said we weren't bringing one, so."

"Where're those?" She nods toward his beer.

The man looks at the bottle as if surprised by its appearance in his hand. "Think there's a cooler maybe up near the turnips?"

"Where are the turnips?"

"Or radishes, maybe? I dunno the difference."

Vee walks toward where he seemed to have gestured in his vague way, walks into the increasingly dense and overgrown farm, holding the present Magi-at-the-manger-like. She holds it delicately not because its content is delicate but because she heard it jostling around on the bumpy drive over and she wants to make sure that it's right-side-up when Charlie opens it. It's a dinosaur, an amphicoelias, often mistaken for a brontosaurus, but so much more massive. This one, though, the one in the box, is about a foot long, plastic—or, rather, acrylic lucite.

She can hear the cheers of children coming in waves from a little glen just down from the apple trees.

The Family Farm, as Pam and Geoff have dubbed their backyard, began as an empty lot behind their house. When Vee first visited, Pam looked out the window at the lot and made a few joking-but-probably-not comments about seeing derelicts in the trees. This was when the cops had begun clearing out camps of homeless, an ongoing game of Whack-A-Mole, the homeless then popping up in another habitable area that the cops would soon clear, and so on, and so Pam's lobbying Geoff to buy up that half-acre lot and farm the shit out of it as an extended backyard, properly fenced-in, didn't seem to be entirely out of horticultural passion.

The yard, The Family Farm, starts close to the house with a modest patch of microgreens, then quickly escalates, sloping up to one side, up to where highland crops like chard and sunflowers and big anonymous leafy things dominate, then retreats back away from the house into a dense cluster of fruit trees, cleft by this glen that looks like it has been carved by a river but surely is just a trick of landscaping. There's a chicken coop somewhere, though she can't see it. Much of the yard she can't see; it seems designed to hide itself, jutting out from Pam and Geoff's California bungalow. Or at least she's always had that impression; she can't actually see its borders.

She keeps heading toward the trees, the highland beyond. An eddy of children swirl around her feet, almost knock her down. She searches them for towheaded Charlie, but all their heads are shades of tow, the whole of Pam's social circle blindingly white.

One child stops while the rest scurry off. He clings to her leg, leans against it like it's a lamppost, to catch his breath.

"Hi," she says.

The boy looks up, slightly annoyed that this lamppost is alive.

"Do you know where Charlie is? I have a birthday present for him." She hears the tone of her voice; she hears how, without meaning to, she's slipped up an octave, a bit bouncy but still gentle. She sounded in that moment like her old roommate the poet did at coffee house readings, all of a sudden the owner of a new voice more fit to the Teletubbies' universe than this one.

The boy, perhaps frightened, runs away.

Vee's bra is hurting her. Underwire must have been invented at Guantanamo. She hates her sweat. With boobs and belly, she always sweats through T-shirts in disturbingly facial patterns, her shirts always looking like nightmares of clown faces. Not the best look for a child's birthday party.

She's walking, present in hand, toward a pocket of kid-noise, over to where the guy with the backpack seemed to have been pointing—radish territory, or turnip. She's not entirely sure either. Even though her knowledge of veg-life is based entirely on her year-long stint waiting tables in one of those rustic farm-to-face eateries, some of the things Pam and Geoff grow here she's totally clueless on. Some of this flora seems like it belongs more in Jurassic Park than in North Berkeley. Leaves the size of her face. Flowers that look sentient.

That Pam inherited their mom's green thumb has always been something of a thing. In college, Pam once

4

said that she was the "producer of food-commodity, while you, Colleen, are the consumer," basically a Marxist fat joke. Now, Pam only brings up her green thumb as a burden, the burden of bearing not just the bountiful womb but the bountiful garden as well. So many obligations, and without her so many things would wither—right, as if the bitch's teat supplies the seven seas. Besides, Pam's are b-cups at best, the bulimic.

Vee finds a little girl standing by herself near the louche plumage of Pam and Geoff's lettuce. Her blonde hair is in a French braid and she is just staring into the air, her limbs and face faintly animated like those of someone deep in dream, doing nothing in that way kids have that seems so active and full, like she's deep in some philosophical debate with an imaginary friend.

Vee stands at a safe distance, as if afraid to wake a sleepwalker. "Scuse me, little girl. Have you seen Charlie?"

The girl turns and eyes Vee's shoes.

"Where's the birthday boy?" Vee asks.

"What color are your shoes?" the girl asks.

Vee looks down. She's wearing the white Chuck Taylors she Magic-Markered into a splotchy black one insomniac night last month. "They're... black and white."

The girl finally looks up at Vee. "Did you scribble on them?"

"I did!"

The girl eyes the present. "Is that for me?"

"No," Vee says. "But you know who it is for?"

"Me?"

"It's for *Charlie*!" Vee says, hearing her voice do the thing again, this time with even more maniacal glee. "The

5

birthday boy!"

The girl suddenly looks like she's just been scolded, and yes, perhaps Vee's awareness of her own demented-clown timbre only kicked it up a frightening notch rather than tempering it.

The girl's chin starts to quiver, her eyes get glassy. Now Vee's on damage control. She crouches down, sets the present beside her. This she can do—it has an explicit goal: keep all teary material from breaching lid or lash.

Saying one word to these kids, it's like leaning against a stranger's Mercedes without the alarm going off. Keeping them from going off, attracting the ire and scorn from these helicopter bitches here, it takes finesse. Vee has finesse; Vlad said so.

"There, there," she says. "There, there." She hugs the child, pats her back. "It's okay." The child does not hug back; she remains, stubbornly and stickly, still. Perhaps Vee's initiation of physical contact was misguided. Perhaps she's doing something *wrong* with this child. She lets go, leans back. The girl's crying situation hasn't technically breached, but some of her lashes are clumped together and beaded by single drops that could, at any second, fall.

"Are you okay?"

"Is that present for me?"

Vee lifts her sleeve to the girl's eyes—she doesn't flinch—and lets the fabric absorb the threatening tears.

"Your hair looks so pretty," Vee says. "How do you get it to do that?"

"Mommy."

"It's very cool."

"Can I have the present?"

"Tell you what," Vee says. "If you help me find Charlie,

I can get you an even better gift."

"What?"

"Something—else."

"Let me see it first."

"You want to see it?"

"Yes."

Vee fishes around in the pocket of her Army surplus jacket, hoping to find some loose cash. Kids love cash. When Vee was nine, she horded dollar bills in a rubber-banded stack under her mattress. She'd seen countless movies in which stacks of cash like this were objects of criminal desire. She didn't care for the money's extrinsic purchasing power; rather, she thought of paper money as possessing a purely intrinsic value of an almost mystical potency. With cash, as Vlad has pointed out, becoming increasingly less concrete and more abstract, mere ones and zeros on a bank's computer screen, it might actually be kind of wonderful to see this child here imbue some simple crumpled up dollar bills with that old magic again. So—despite Vlad's continued admonishment of adults who resort to bribery with children, despite his avowal that when they have kids they'll never do that—right?—because they'll be cool parents, and despite the ovarian twitch of terror and joy and God-knows what other primitive procreative shit Vee felt when he mentioned the two of them having kids—she fishes for dollars in the pocket of her Army surplus jacket.

She doesn't, however, find any cash.

Instead, her fingers wrap around the blown-glass one-hitter, still warm from the hit she took in the car before coming into the party.

"Well?" the girl says.

Vee takes the little glass pipe out of her pocket and holds it up.

The girl seems transfixed, her mouth agape like Vee were holding an Oreo an inch from her mouth. "It's beautiful," she says.

And it is. Smooth and bulbous at one end, patterned with a swirl of glistening granite, striped with a deep malachite green, it looks like a small alien's penis. Vee bought it for five bucks on Telegraph sometime in high school, and in anxious moments often rubs it in her pocket like a worry stone.

The girl reaches for the pipe and Vee pulls it away. "Only if you help me find Charlie."

The girl tightens her lips, clenches her face into a look of resolve. She turns around with militant precision, and starts marching. Vee follows.

They pass by bushes the size of discontinued Eastern European cars that smell oddly like massage oil. They pass large brown paper bags filled with clippings and dead leaves. They pass a fresh, unplanted garden bed filled with a dark loam of fertilizer and mulch and what Vee recognizes, or thinks she recognizes, as corners of biodegradable diapers emerging from the soil like shark fins from water. But surely Charlie is shitting like an adult by now, right?

The girl is getting faster. When Vee turns a corner, she only sees the end of the girl's braid disappearing around the next corner of aggressive flora. Vee breaks into a trot to keep up, to catch up, but then she stops, because of her boobs. She worries they look like speedbags when she runs.

The girl's now entirely out of sight. Vee hears a scuffling of shoes with a kid-like rhythm on the other side of this freakish bush here with canoe-shaped leaves, but it turns out to be some totally other kid, a boy sucking on his lower lip and tugging—exploratorily but determinedly—at his pecker through his shorts. Vee asks him, "You seen a girl run by here with a French braid?"

The boy shakes his head and continues his tugging, to which Vee leaves him.

That quick little sprint has winded her. She couldn't even say a simple sentence to that boy without stopping every few words for air.

She needs some water.

The cooler by the turnips, or radishes, is full of fancy beer, a microbrew whose label has a steampunk sensibility. Vee puts the present down by her feet so she can open a bottle with the church-key yarned to the cooler. She takes a drink. The booze boasts notes of pinecones and patchouli.

The dad with the backpack walks up, aerodynamic sunglasses now giving his face a Terminator-ish look.

"One of these ankle-biters yours?" the man asks.

"Charlie," Vee says.

One of the man's eyebrows crests over his Oakleys.

"I'm his aunt."

Now the other eyebrow goes up.

"I'm Vee."

"Oh," the man says, lowering his eyebrows. "I hear a bunch about another sister, Colleen, down in Oakland."

"West Oakland, yeah."

"Pam was nervous she'd show up. Or that's what my wife said. What's her deal?" The man thumbs up the brim of his hat; its yellow fabric has grown a green crown of sweat.

"Want a beer?" Vee says.

"Uh-huh."

She pulls a second bottle from the cooler, melty ice-bits sliding down its neck, opens it. She tries to hand him the beer, but he says, "Hold on." He unloops one shoulder of his backpack, unvelcroes a compartment built to hold a pack of baby-wipes. He pulls out one baby-wipe, and a new one flowers up in its place. He wipes his hands clean, then pulls a Ziploc baggie from his pocket, puts the used wipe inside, zippers it shut, and puts it back into his pocket.

Then he says, "Name's Floyd," and holds out his hand.

Vee shakes his hand and instantly realizes he was holding it out to accept the beer. She takes her hand back and gives him the beer.

A woman walks up in hair fit for a yacht club, nicotine tan and velveteen jumper. "Floyd," she says, "where's Skylar's toque? There's a chill and it's getting cold tonight."

She begins rustling through Floyd's backpack. He doesn't seem to pay much attention, like a pack horse.

"You look knowledgeable," Vee says to the woman.

The woman huffs. "I better be."

"Do you know where I can put my present? For Charlie? Or do you know where he is?"

She finds the toque, pulls it out. It looks like one of the Wicked Witch's stockings. "This isn't a present party, honey. And Charlie? I think I saw him over by the nopales."

"What are nopales?"

"They're near the salsify bush."

"Oh. Right."

Beer in one hand, present lodged under her other arm, Vee wanders away in an uncommitted direction.

She sees the tree-house, and the edge of the fruit-tree district, and heads toward it. It's the tree-house she herself built four years ago, just before Charlie was born. But she built it on a feeble cottonwood tree—the largest tree they had on the property at that point, before they imported all these large, load-bearing oaks with their gnarled muscly roots—and the resulting tree-house is less a residence, less the Swiss-Family-Robinson-style chalet she'd imagined, and more a simple platform, about four feet by four feet, big enough only for one person to sit, solo.

Pam is standing under the tree-house.

"Charlie play on that much?" Vee asks.

Pam looks up from her phone, sees Vee and makes a face: a smile or smelling something strange, you can never tell with Pam. She says, "Hiya."

Vee hugs Pam, but Pam's phone-holding hand gets caught, bent T-Rex-like between the sisters' bodies.

"Where's the birthday boy?"

"We don't let him up there," Pam says. "It doesn't seem stable. Geoff wants to take it down."

"Where should I put this?" Vee holds up the present.

"Besides, there're nails sticking out up there. Tetanus. Lockjaw."

"Where should I put my gift? For Charlie?"

"What's that?"

"Where's Charlie?"

Pam says, "Um, Colleen, we said no gifts? In the invite? Big as can be? Did you not see it?"

"What? Why? Where's Charlie? My name is Vee now. Not Colleen."

A small child, one of the not-Charlies, runs by cradling a chicken in his arms, the animal's feathery head twitching

11

nervously.

"Hey!" Pam shouts with sudden anger, at Vee or at the kid it's momentarily unclear. "Declan! Come back here, Declan! Put Roosevelt down!"

The kid tries to scurry into a garden bed of unidentifiable flora, but he trips. He lands on Roosevelt and the chicken lets out a chilling squawk, and the kid's butt—red shorts hiding crinkling diapers—is left sticking skyward. Pam grabs the boy by the waist, pulls him off Roosevelt. The chicken runs into the wilderness.

"Geoff and I made it clear at Christmas," Pam shouts back at Vee while slapping the dirt off the boy's shirt. "No gifts. We want Charlie to understand that the real gifts are family, friends, and fellowship, not gross material possessions." She points the child away, swats his butt, and he runs off. "Besides, Geoff and I provide him with whatever he wants anyway. Really, Colleen, we made it very clear in the Evite. Don't you read?"

The tinselly ribbon on the gift reflects the sunlight, making flashes in Vee's peripheral vision like she has another detached retina.

"My name's Vee now."

"No it's not."

"It is," she says. "Legally."

"Colleen, you've never done anything legally." Pam begins, or continues, to do something on her phone, scrolling her thumbs against the screen as if massaging the thing.

"Where's Charlie?"

Pam looks up annoyed. "Colleen. I'm really stressed out right now. The protests downtown? I have CitiWatch to update, *while* running this party. I should be an octopus for all the arms I need right now. So can you just answer your questions on your own, thanks."

Pam stomps off.

Vee feels hyperventilative again, now without the inconvenience of running. She guzzles the rest of her beer, lets out a painful and heartburn-spiced burp. She pushes her thumb into the mouth of the bottle until it hurts. She wishes she had Vlad's extroverted sense for destruction, could just throw a bottle against a wall and feel exorcised of all shit. Instead, she just keeps pushing her thumb knuckle in until it feels like something, bone or bottle, will break.

She pulls her thumb out and the tip is purple, ringed painfully at the knuckle in white. She tosses the bottle into a plumage of swiss chard, then panics that there might be some kid hiding there to get knocked in the head by her carelessness. She can't even throw a bottle right, not without having an aneurysm of guilt about the poor bottle's feelings.

Back up in the turnip or radish clearing, Floyd is still standing beside the cooler, now with his backpack unzipped, slackly letting diapers and sweaters flap in the wind.

Vee sets the present down and grabs a second beer.

"How much do you think these things cost?" she asks Floyd.

"Thirty-five-something for a case," Floyd says.

"That's remarkably specific."

"We brought 'em. Made a Costco run on the way. Got five pounds of frozen tortellini defrosting in the trunk."

"Your wife said it's getting cold."

"Yeah, well, she sleeps with tube socks on her hands in ninety-degree weather."

Vee starts in on the second beer, taking big frothy mouthfuls that feel like they continue to froth in her stomach.

"Slow down there," Floyd says.

Thirty-five-something for a case of twenty-four beers, plus CRV, means, what, around a buck-fifty per?

"I can't," she says. "I need to drink twenty-two ninety-five worth of beer."

Floyd nods. "Gotcha."

"Fuck acrylic lucite," Vee says.

Floyd looks away. "That's what I always say."

That kid, what's his name, Declan, the same one who tried to kidnap Roosevelt—or maybe this is a different kid but same make and model—is suddenly rooting around Vee's feet. Just as Vee registers the kid's identity, he grabs the gift and runs off, so simply, into the controlled wild of his sister's absurd backyard, gone.

Vee shouts—a vowely something, gurgley with beer, or perhaps a simple choking sound. Then, foaming bottle in hand, she runs after, boob-show be damned.

The path is brier-clotted and the boy's Keds kick up dirt and dust like a smokescreen of diesel exhaust. Vee's foot catches on the half-buried wood slat of a garden bed's border, and she plants face-first into some hard vegetable. She feels a bristly something scraping her belly where her shirt has hitched up and her sleeve is now soaked with beer. She landed, she sees now, in a broccoli plant. The veggie isn't as soft as she expected it to be, and she realizes it has been a while since she's had it any way other than steamed and covered in cheddar.

There's the sound of kid-laughter around her, many kids, all reveling in that sociopathic part of their development. It's a horrible, discordant clang, the laughter more an aggressive communication of dominance than a genuine bubbling up of pleasure.

By the time she stands up the gang is already running off, only their conical party hats visible over the vegetation.

That guy at the toy store yesterday, a college-age kid, suggested a toy marked "2 - 4 yrs." He was one of these skinny boys whose sweater-vest and thick-rimmed glasses only function to make his devastating good looks seem accidental.

He asked, "Who's this for?"

She said she wanted to get her nephew a birthday gift, one that she could play with too. "We have similar sensibilities, him and I."

He chuckled, adjusted his frames. "That's funny." His smile went from the head-on variety of customer service to the oblique, head-cocked variety of flirtation. "So you play with him a lot?"

"Yes, of course," she said. "We're very close."

"And what sort of things does he like?"

She hates those questions. They're impossible. Like the question that used to be on her online dating profile that asked her what she liked to do for fun. Who knew how to answer that? Everything always sounds false. Online, she'd left that question, and others, blank, in part hoping to normalize the blankness of her employment status, but here, with a real live person, she had to come up with something.

"He likes pooping, mostly."

The toy store boy laughed again.

"And he," she said, "you know, likes to gum things."

"But you said he's turning four—wouldn't he be done teething by now?"

Maybe. Charlie could also be out of diapers by now. But it still counted as a good joke. She'd had a good four seconds of flirtation—or what she considered flirtation. Why'd he have to ruin it by being so literal minded? She had to more clearly establish joke territory. "Well, you certainly seem pretty concerned about teething. Don't worry, honey, I've got good technique—all lips and tongue."

In the moment it took for his face to register the joke, she panicked, worried that she'd just sexually harassed the guy. But then he smiled, chortled, and said, "Yes, well." He finished the sentence by needlessly adjusting his frames again.

It's not that she was attracted to him—or rather, she *was* attracted to him, but that wasn't why she'd attempted any sort of flirtation, no matter how maniacal it came out. She was just tired of how pretty boys like this always tolerate big girls with a smile, how they can confidently throw a scrap of flirt her way as if it's charity—yes, good for you, pat on the back—because to them a fat chick is never a sexual possibility, is always and completely unthreatening.

This bit of sexual aggression wasn't a betrayal of Vlad; it was an assault on this kid's skinny privilege.

Fuck it: "But I only go quid pro quo, so I hope you got good tongue technique." She winked. His face went flat and either he raised his shoulders or sunk slightly into them as if into a turtle shell. "I think someone's at the front counter. Just give a call if you need anything else."

He simpered off.

And that's when she saw it, the dinosaur, the amphicoelias, on an endcap shelf otherwise littered with plush pugs. The noble beast of the Late Jurassic misplaced amongst the genetic freaks of Late Capitalism. She walked over and picked up the amphicoelias, the subtle curve of its long body. It had a nice heft to it, smooth, about the length of her forearm. She's always loved dinosaurs, all kinds, but the amphicoelias, it was her favorite. Often mistaken for brontosauruses because of their shape, but she knew. As a kid, she'd memorized the amphicoelias's classifications, the whole deal—family, genus, species—but most impressive was their sheer size—incomprehensible—an average of a hundred and forty tons, from nose to tail-tip stretching two-thirds of a football field, so huge that to truly contemplate it had been to get a terrifying lesson in scale, to realize the smallness of her own hundred-pound existence. She had since more than doubled that poundage, but standing now in the toy store, holding the quarter-pound plastic model, she still felt a pang of insignificance, the odd comfort of that, and she surprised herself by still being able to reel off the dinosaur's classifications, a melody forever crinkled into her frontal cortex.

During her year of college, she'd spent many nights getting high with the amphicoelias skeleton mounted outside the Vertebrate Lab Museum. She would climb over the cable fence and position herself lotus-legged below the cage of the creature's ribs, a Jonah who had no intention of escaping the beast's belly. Above, the glass-shard glimmer in the sky's dense fabric was barred by the creature's ribs, everything—stars and bone—exposed in opalescent conversation.

"That's five and up," the toy store guy said when she brought the dinosaur up to the counter. He was intensely scrutinizing the cash register and the toy's tag to avoid eye contact.

She looked at the tag. "Twenty-two dollars?"

"Well, it *is* acrylic lucite," the guy said. "But really, this is for ages five and up. Choking hazard."

"Oh, please," she said. "How could anyone choke on this?"

One night in college, she showed up and found a small gang of students already squatting in her spot, gathered around a case of Keystone Light. They had flashlights, flared them around like lightsabers. One saw her, called out with an invitation that was ostensibly nice but had a definite *suwee* tone. She knew that tone. She took off, up into the hills, clutching her glass-blown pipe in her hoodie's kangaroo pocket. A short hike up, hidden and barbed off by bushes, there was a bluff where a small tributary ran thin like cellophane over the rocks. She followed it to a lagoon populated by large, carbuncular rock formations. To one side, she could see the overwhelming expanse of the Pacific, the moonlight moving on the waves like stars come to life. In the other direction, she had a view of the small cityscape, which had been growing this past year like a losing game of Tetris. The lagoon had the appearance of something untouched by anything human, but it was surely just another lab for tagging and testing. In the morning, students would arrive, take samples, catalogue.

Two.

Most of the chickens seem skittish, just flocking together near the blueberry bush. Roosevelt, however, is brave. She recognizes him from the spats-like covering of white feathers on his feet, dignified. He steps forward and jabs his head around Vee's feet. But when she crouches down and reaches out, slowly, to pet the bird, the thing turns and skottles off.

"Asshole." She stands up, and Roosevelt scurries down the root-gnarled path. The rest of the chickens follow.

Vee holds the empty but still-cold beer bottle against her forearm, which was scraped raw in her tumble, and follows the pack of chickens. Or no, not pack. A pride of chickens? A murder of chickens? A parliament? Probably nothing that cool. One of her favorite books from kidhood was called *An Exaltation of Larks*, which catalogued, illustrated, and held forth on all those various terms of venery. It was written by that loon who later hosted *Inside the Actors Studio*, and was full of a bizarre kind of whimsy that was so utterly foreign to her family that it seemed animated by a demented magic. It's the same kind of energy that fills Vlad after watching *Monty Python*, and although Vee never quite laughs with him in this mode—which always seems to break his heart a bit—she is always, in her way, enthralled. She wishes she still had that book, a lot of things.

The chickens lead her to their coop, tucked beneath an orange tree slung with a small tire swing.

The coop is a corrugated metal construction that looks like the cabin her old roommate recently posted photos of online, claiming to have built. The ex-roommate even captioned the photos with tales of her rugged self-reliance and Thoreau quotes with creative phonetic spellings to fit into 140 characters.

This construction does look pretty swank to house a bunch of flightless land birds. Here, on their own territory, the chickens seem less jittery. She walks through them to the laddered ramp that has a Skee-Ball look to it. She leans over the ramp and pokes her head into the coop itself. There's only one chicken inside, sitting on her perch, looking righteous and grandmotherly. Each bird seems to have her own cubbyhole, plenty of room in the middle for socializing. Reminds her a little of that artists' live-work space Vlad lived in when they first met.

Suddenly she feels a slap on her ass followed by an explosion of kid-laughter. She jerks up and hits the back of her head on the coop's doorframe. In the awful moment before the pain hits, she's able to remove her head from the coop, turn and then—the pain hitting—see four or five of them, the kids, in amongst the chickens. The one—kid, that is—who's out front, the one whose hand is still half-cocked in the air and surely responsible for the petite-size slap she felt, his face is frozen. He seems unsure whether his stunt will be met with punishment or laughter.

"Pin the tail on the donkey!" the others shout behind him, and they all start squealing. "Pin the tail on the donkey!"

The lead boy spazzes with excitement. He's wearing a Metallica T-shirt ironically tyke-size, and has a blonde mop-top beneath a bright blue party hat with a silvery diamond pattern on it.

Vee, harnessing the energy and indignation the

throbbing in her head is giving her, grabs the slapper by the shoulder, and his face goes drama-mask scared. The rest of his gang quiets. The aura of trouble, the trouble they're in. Doesn't matter that she doesn't know these kids; her being an adult is all the authority she needs to cow them.

"Listen," she says, calm but forceful. "I'm looking for Declan." Is that his name? Something that sounds like a mispronunciation of another name, or a deck sealant. "Do you guys know Declan?"

They all nod: success.

"Declan has a box," she says, still gripping the boy's bony arm, "and it's my box. I need that box back. I need you to find him and that box and bring him to me."

"What do we get if we do?" says one girl in the gang.

"Jesus, you're a bunch of capitalists, aren't you. Okay." She fishes in her pocket, pulls out the pipe again. "You see this? Pretty, right?"

She's holding the pipe up and their eyes are all locked on it.

"What is it?" that girl asks.

"It's pretty and shiny and smooth, that's what it is," Vee says.

She shoves the pipe back in her pocket, quickly disappears it in a way she hopes will inspire them to swift and merciless action.

"Remember," she says. "Declan. You're looking for Declan. But he's worthless to me without that box. Got it?"

They all nod confirmation.

"Okay," she says, "disperse!"

And they do, remarkably. Her minions, her flying monkeys, scatter into the backyard.

She hears a distant machine-gun sound above her. She looks up. It's just a helicopter moving across the late afternoon sky. Surely to the protests downtown. They've been growing by the day, all month, all century.

She walks back up the path, up the little hill out of the Valley of the Chickens, and finds herself at a garden bed recognizable for its bunch of spindly blueberry bushes. Retracing her steps, though some of those steps were not steps at all but rather footless tumbles, she walks back up— up past the tomato plants holding their blood-red fruit like embarrassing growths, up past the avocado tree with its teardrop offerings—to the beer cooler in the radish- or turnip-encircled clearing.

She grabs another beer, does some quick math to see how many more she'll have to drink before balancing out the cost of the gift her asshole sister won't let her give Charlie, then pops the top and lets the bottle-cap flip off into the dirt.

It feels good, the cold beer irrigating her chest.

She feels a slight rustling on her ass, where that kid slapped her, and she turns to see a man standing beside her. He's a young guy with a soul-patch and a French-waxed moustache, and he's holding a length of brown fabric in his hand. "Sorry," he says, "didn't mean to startle you. I don't normally go around picking things off other people's butts. It just looks like the 'pin the tail on the donkey' kids got you."

"Oh," she says, placing a hand where the kid slapped her.

"Don't worry," he says, "you weren't the only one donkeyed."

Either his smile is creepy or it's just his moustache

22

that makes everything he says feel like she needs to check Urban Dictionary for its intended meaning.

"Luckily Pam and Geoff got Velcro tails. I was at one of these parties a few months ago where the kids had tails with thumb-tacks."

"Jesus."

"Yeah, the birthday girl's grandma had to go to the hospital for tetanus. Lockjaw set in."

He's looking at her. She drinks her beer. He watches her drink her beer like a parent making sure she takes her medicine. Then he says, "I should get one of those too," and reaches into the cooler for one.

"I'm Ryan," he says, puts out his hand.

She shakes it, its moisturized white-collaredness. "Vee."

"Hi, Vee." He swigs his beer, strains drops from his moustache with his lower lip. "We've met before, right?"

She rolodexes his face, can't find a match. "I don't think so."

"I think we have," he says. He pets his chin puff. "Are you involved in CitiWatch?"

"No."

"You come to Pam and Geoff's things often?"

"No, not really," she says. "Not in a while."

"Hmmm," he says, as if scanning her.

This sort of thing happened more when she was on that dating website. Guys would approach her, in a bar, in line at the grocery store, having surely recognized her from her profile but unwilling to either say that or flirt with her through the approved and appropriate means established by the website. These were typically guys whom she imagined had stalked her profile because they had a big-girl fetish but were too embarrassed to do anything about it, so they were reduced to ultimately impotent and creepy conversations like this. There's always a tone of expectation and even entitlement in these conversations. The assumed desperation of being on a dating website infinitely compounds the assumed desperation of being a big girl, which means these guys approach her like she's standing on the side of the road wearing a sandwich board that says, "Will Give Head for Eye Contact and Minimal Conversation," with a small-print footnote ensuring she won't tell your friends you fucked a fat chick.

She handles Ryan The Moustache here the same way she handled the rest, kindly bids him well and walks away. She hasn't been on that dating website for—what? Almost a year? No, she met Vlad just before Christmas, so eight months. She worries that her profile might still be accidentally up there, or cached or somehow accessible. She's done with the creepers it brought out, has officially retired from being a fetish object.

Still, she prefers those guys, the ones who just haven't faced up to liking big girls yet, over the ones who actually did contact her on that website.

There was that guy who took her out for drinks, artisanal cocktails at his friend's bar. He seemed perfectly lovely in his way with his white-boy Orientalist tattoos of koi ponds and dragons. He said he was a refugee from San Francisco's escalating costs and was working on developing an app that would locate microbreweries in your immediate vicinity. "Geotagging is where it's at," he said.

"That sounds like what biologists do to wildlife," she said.

"I don't get it." And then he took her back to his place

and after they made out a while and he got her shirt off, he went over to his laptop and started setting up a webcam. When she declined participation, he called an Uber to take her home.

There was the guy who smelled like Dove soap with the shaggy hair who after two dates took her home and eschewed vaginal or even oral sex for lubing up her stomach and sliding his dick across and into its lateral fat fold. Vee, then Colleen, a pillow propped behind her head, just watched this dude copulate ecstatically with her belly. She felt neither pleasure nor pain in this, just curiosity, began seeing his sex-spazzed rabbit-like thrusting as if through the wrong end of a telescope. This guy, this boy, having such a passionate experience with a part of her body that simply lacked the appropriate nerve endings to allow her equal engagement, made her feel like her body, her flesh, was nothing more than a costume of a character whom she no longer was.

There was the guy, the guy whose wedding-ring tan-line he rubbed the whole night, who asked her on their first date if she was into feederism. When she said she wasn't sure what that was, he didn't offer a definition. But she began to get a general idea when he steered her away from the salad with a vehement endorsement of the deep-fried cheese-stuffed chili peppers and began to look aroused when she took her first tentative bites.

She follows the sound of adult conversation back toward the calm steppe of microgreens, figures she'll hide for a moment in an awkward adult circle of idle chat. She finds just the circle she expected and slides in unnoticed. Pam and Geoff are positioned at opposite ends of the group, as if to kettle the conversation.

"It's just the anger," one lady is saying, holding her hands to her chest as if afraid her blouse will fly off in a gust of wind. "It's not helpful. I mean, Martin Luther King wasn't angry. Not that I met the guy, but he seemed really lovely."

"Well," says the man beside her, "invoking Dr. King would suggest this is about race and economics and, you know, civil rights, which is just—" He pauses to massage his beard, searching for a conclusion to his diagnosis in there amongst the scone crumbs. "You know, just false. This is really about—what this is about is—is just the, listen—I mean, did you see the level of property destruction? I mean, the cost of that? To taxpayers?"

"Vandalism," Pam pipes up. "That's all it is."

"Thank you, by the way." This from a new lady, looking fresh from a marathon in sweat-wicking running gear and a safety-pinned number. "We had to re-plan our route at the crack of dawn this morning and we were so dependent on your CitiWatch updates. Your tracking the movements of those—protesters, thugs, whatever they are. Had it not been for you, our runners might have gone through what's now a ghetto!"

The beard-comber says, "Places, streets, that just yesterday, the day before, seemed perfectly calm."

"Thank you," Pam says. "That's what makes it all worth it, hearing from people like you. I'm trying, you know. I'm just doing my best."

"Did you all hear?" Geoff says. "Pam's getting recognized by the *Chronicle*."

A collective gasp of awe and curiosity from the group.

"What can I say?" Pam says, demurring. "When it rains

it pours." She gives a chuckle of satisfaction. No one gets more pleasure out of validating personal anecdotes with a quick confirmation of cliché, no one more than Pam. She's happiest when she can sand the edges off experience, slide it neatly into well-vetted language.

Geoff says, "They're calling it the most innovative community activist campaign in the Bay."

"Well, *yeah*," the marathoner says. "I mean, social media!"

"It's all about geotagging," Pam says. "Really, Geoff is such a great champion," holding her hand up as if to shield the glare of adoration. "We haven't announced it on the site yet because we're waiting until they run the story on Sunday. But, yes."

"Bravo," a new man says, "bravo," and initiates a round of applause. Most clap a hand against their forearm because their other hand is holding a drink.

Vee skips the clapping and goes straight to the drinking.

"My modest contribution," Pam says, surely citing their father and his often slurred insistence that they *contribute*—though contribute to what he didn't seem to care. This was one of many such proclamations made in his single-parent desperation to provide declarative life lessons, clear prescriptions for the self in society. "I've even been contacted by the Berkeley Police Commissioner," Pam says, "to coordinate efforts."

"Oh, how *is* Dwight?" says the bravo man.

"He's doing great."

Someone not doing great, however, someone back deep in the yard, rents the air with a scream high-pitched enough to be gender-ambiguous. No one screams like a kid, no one else can stretch a single note into such a barbed

27

and fissured thing, an alarm designed for rupture.

The moms in the crowd snap into super-mom mode. Spines straighten, arms angle to wrangle herds of babes. With no visible object for their energy, they spend a moment fussing around, competing amongst each other for the more furious display of determination and capability. Then Pam, vanguard Pam, she runs into the yard with the confidence only someone familiar with its insane layout can. The rest follow—dads included—shouting after their various ill-named issue.

Vee follows too. Though she hates this self-righteous mutual appreciation society, she appreciates the invisibility they offer her when she's tired of being seen.

The parade of parents leads her to a garden bed of leeks where Declan, that thieving shit Declan, stands like a monument of sorrow in the center of these people's attention, sobbing with such naïve conviction that the world cares.

This small world, however, does.

A woman steps forward. Lean, made of unholy angles and serrated looks, she tends performatively to what is presumably her child. The boy seems to have a few raw pink blurs across his forearms, not unlike the markings this very kid caused Vee when she fell into the broccoli.

The mom, cheating more toward the audience than the child, says, "Who did this to you? Who? Are you okay? Who did this?"

The boy, sniveling between desperate gasps of breath, his voice clogged and bubbled with snot, says, "Waylon!" And then Declan points into the bushes, where that kid, the one who slapped Vee's ass, presumably pinning the donkey tail on her, apparitions in the mess of rutabaga greens. Waylon's looking scared, wearing a look of guilt and eager repentance. He nervously adjusts his blue and silver party hat.

Pam leads a swarm of parents to Waylon. On bended knees they demand to know—caringly, achingly—*what happened.*

Before Waylon can offer his version of events, Declan, wiping away viscous snot-tears from his face, says, "He hit me! He hit me! He stole my present!"

"Present?" Pam demands. "*Your* present? What is this talk of first-person possessives? There are no presents here. *What* present?"

"I got it from *her!*" Declan points a dirty fingernail directly at Vee.

The adults throw eye-daggers at her like she's made of magnet.

"No," Vee says. "I don't know—" But she stops there.

Pam rises from her concerned crouch, walks toward Vee.

Vee reaches in her pocket and rubs the one-hitter for comfort.

Pam passes right by Vee and goes back to Declan, grabs his arm. She holds the tender red elbow up and shouts at Vee, "See? Do you see what your materialism has wrought? Do you *see?*"

Vee feels it, the tingling tremor of tears in her sinuses. She can't cry in front of others. As a policy. She bites her lip, hard.

Declan's mom scoops up the boy and asks Pam, "Where's your Bactine?"

"The master bathroom," Pam says.

"I'll show you," Geoff says.

"No!" Pam says. Then she turns back to Vee. "Colleen's going to show you where the bathroom is. She's going to help minister to Declan's wounds."

Vee can taste blood.

Pam turns and storms away, the rest of the parents quickly parting for her to pass through.

Declan's mom, her son resting his head on her breast in what looks like a muscle memory of breastfeeding, walks toward the house, its roof just visible above the ficus.

Vee follows at a reasonable distance, keeping her eyes fixed on the rectangular outline of the cellphone in the lady's back pocket, like it's the focal object in a meditation exercise. Just stare at this one fixed spot and let everything else fall away. Vee has done this successfully only once, the whole awful rest of the world slipping into a blur, but she was on DMT at the time, and the technique is working considerably less well now. Maybe this lady's butt isn't staying still enough to be a proper meditation focal point.

The butt suddenly stops and its owner turns around.

"Listen," she says. "Colleen, is it?"

"No."

"Well, Colleen, you don't really need to come do this. I got it, okay? You don't need to show me where the bathroom is or swab Bactine on Declan's arm." Declan, whose blank face suggests he's already neatly suppressed his recent trauma, is now idly pushing his tiny mitt into her boob. "I appreciate Pam's a little irked at you, but it's not cool of her to farm out my parenting duties as punishment for someone else. Besides, Declan's sensitive to disinfectants and I have a special technique so it'd be best if you didn't even try."

She carries Declan away, off toward the house.

Back at the avocado tree, a little later, seemingly alone, Vee plucks an avocado off a branch. She holds it in her hand. She's never known the secrets of the mystical gropings of the farmers-market frequenters—those white-bearded white dudes, pant-legs cuffed for biking, picking up produce, divining from bulbous things with squeezings and sniffings some significance inaccessible to everyone else. Whenever she buys produce it turns out to be unripe or browning.

She holds this avocado in her hand. Its—what?—flesh?—its flesh is remarkably fleshy. Like what she imagines dinosaur flesh to be like. Tough, rivet-studded, but still responsive, receptive to touch.

She's never understood the Californian obsession with avocados, has always felt like her aversion to them is a mark against her claim to citizenship. To be fair, they're pleasant to hold like this, with the pebbly skin protecting you from the awful interior, but once you cut in you feel like a Civil War doctor sawing into a gangrenous leg.

Their father, hers and Pam's, in his later fits of lunacy, used to eat these things smashed together with brie and white bread, nothing else. Pam tried to ply the man with veggies, the kind of things now terrorizing this very yard, unidentifiable tubers and stalks. He had nothing of it. Would only eat his mushy brie-and-avo sandos.

She hates how easily Pam cows her, cows everyone. The pattern's been there for years: Alone, Vee can rile herself up into righteous indignation about Pam's assholery, think of the perfect things to say to her—beautiful opuses of oration and rhetoric that would bring Pam to her knees, make her apologize for herself and for the world. But then as soon as Pam's there in person, Vee shits the bed and capitulates, returns to her old sad passive self, that teenage self. Illusions of adulthood evaporate in the face of family.

She winds up and hurls the avocado up and away. She doesn't hear it land.

Her beer is empty. The feeling of a beer or bong depleting is like the feeling of the last friend leaving the party, always a small pang of heartbreak and betrayal in the inevitable and awful evidence of entropy. All beers end.

She bends down and prods her fingers into the soft soil around whatever root vegetable this is at her feet. Leaves like the ruffles on an old tuxedo shirt. Down there in the dirt, beneath the surface, she feels the firm root of something. She has the sense that if she could only get her hands around this root, so taut it seems load-bearing, and pull it, snap it loose of its obligations, this whole backyard will fall. Like closing a pop-up book, simple, a whole diorama folding down to sleep.

Vee plants the empty bottle halfway in the dirt, gets up and heads toward where she thinks the clearing with the beer cooler is. Not so much for another beer as because it offers the most orienting—though far from complete—view of the yard. But also because: beer.

As she walks, she hears a slight echo behind her every footfall. She stops. The echo stops. She continues walking. The echo waits a few steps then picks up again. She swings around and sees Waylon. He jumps, then freezes: caught.

"Got another donkey tail you wanna stick to my ass?" Vee says. "Or is it just for a cheap grope?"

Waylon pulls on his little Metallica shirt, now stained with mustard around the collar, and says, "You said to get the present."

"I didn't say thrash that kid and get me in trouble."

"Declan always cries."

"So you should've known to be careful."

"But you said to get the present so I got it."

"And you almost got me fucking banished!"

At the shock of her tone—finally shedding, she realizes, her obsequious kid-friendly tone—the boy shrinks, retreats a little into himself.

"Wait," Vee says. "What did you say? You got the present?"

The kid, now playing silent, nods.

"Well? Where is it?"

The kid just pulls his shirt. Then tentatively points—out there, somewhere behind him.

"There?" she says, pointing along with him, out into the vague whatever.

He nods.

"And just where the fuck is that? Come on, kid, *show* me."

He's now just twisting the hem of his shirt. Staring dumbly at Vee, he lets the twist go to reveal a shattered-glass pattern of wrinkles.

"Turn," she says, pointing with dictatorial certainty. "March. Show me to the treasure!"

This he responds to. Mention of *treasure* seems to unlock a smile, and he turns and starts marching. Remembering how that French-braid girl got away from her, Vee quickly catches up to him, puts a hand on his shoulder. "Heel, heel, there, doggy. Okay, now let's mush—together."

He leads her down a bumpy path flanked by fava bean bushes.

She says, "Did it bother you, Waylon, that I switched

metaphors back there? You know, from the treasure-hunting metaphor to the Iditarod?"

Waylon says, "Okay."

"I know you liked the treasure-hunting gimmick, so we can stick with that if you like."

"Okay."

"Is that just your response to most adult-speak?"

He stops at a cross-street of eggplant and cauliflower. Looks both ways, does some kid-thinking, then turns left, leading them down Cauliflower Lane.

"This is a good system of conversation we have here, Waylon."

"Okay."

"I can just talk the way I usually talk—that is, to myself, for no one's amusement or edification other than my own. I get the benefit of a buddy so I look less insane, without having to deal with that undertow of judgment you usually find in conversations."

"Okay."

"I could tell you anything—secret fear, secret fascination—and your apparatus is simply not developed enough to judge it as ordinary or deviant."

"Okay."

"Let's give this a test-run. I was born with a vestigial tail three feet long and my bedroom is wallpapered with boudoir shots of Abe Vigoda. What do you think about that?"

"Okay."

"You're my kinda man, Waylon."

"Okay."

"I'm terrified of fire. Not little flames in lighters, but anything bigger than that freaks me to the core—intrusive thoughts of immolation."

Waylon stops, hesitates, then climbs off the path into a raspberry patch. The plants are rowed on wooden stakes like at a vineyard. It looks like a delicate and potentially thorny situation in there, so Vee stays on the path, lets her little flying monkey do his thing. Sure enough, he returns, waddling back, box in hands.

"Champion," she says. "You're a goddamn champion."

She takes the present. Wrapping paper a little scuffed, smeared with mud like skid marks on BVDs, but it's still intact.

Waylon taps her thigh.

"What is it, squirt?"

"The prize."

"This is a present, not a prize."

"My prize. You promised me the prize."

He rubs crust from his nose.

"Shit," Vee says. "You're right." She crouches down, sets the present beside her. Remembering how Declan ambushed her, she looks around, sees no one, places a protective knee against the present. She pulls from her pocket the pipe, looks it over. The blackened bits of spent bud inside the bowl, she dumps it out, then cleans the bowl with the sleeve of her jacket.

"I present to you, Waylon, your prize." She hands it to him on her open palm.

His eyes go Keane on the thing, but he doesn't take it. "What is it? What does it do?"

"It's a prize, that's all. It doesn't have to *do* anything. Isn't it just nice?"

"It looks like kryptonite."

"I guess you're kinda right. It's made with a mineral

called malachite. Aren't you impressed that I know that?"

"Okay."

"Have you seen malachite before?"

He nods. "Malachi is the fat boy in my theater camp. He complained that they gave him the Falstaff part because of prejudice against fat people. We did a bunch of plays about a guy named Henry and I got to be him in the last one. I got to have a sword."

"Good enough," Vee says. "Now take your toy."

He does, quickly holds it behind his back as if afraid Vee will snatch it back.

"I mean—not your toy. Your totally unpragmatic object whose value is aesthetic not functional. Got it?"

"Okay."

If Waylon is unwowed, at least Vlad has always been impressed with her knowledge of sciencey minutiae. Their first date, she dropped a reference to the radioactive element Berkelium. Mostly as a joke about the pretensions of her hometown having its own namesake on the periodic table, but Vlad took it as a chance to probe her brain. That's actually what he said: "I wanna probe your brain. You got a lot of stuff boppin' around in there."

"Not too much, really. I was always good with anything that could fit onto a flashcard. But anything that went beyond the borders of a four-by-five… I dunno."

"See, I didn't even do flashcards in school. I just did whippets. Trust me, if you can make it rain science words like—you know, like they're Benjamins at a strip club. You follow me? I mean, you could get onto *Jeopardy!* or something."

"Yeah, well, while I get on *Jeopardy!*, my sister gets

master's degrees. She's the smart one. Some people, their brains are like *Moby-Dick*. But my brain, I feel my brain is like the dictionary. All the words that are in *Moby-Dick* are also in the dictionary, mostly, but the dictionary sure as fuck ain't *Moby-Dick*, you know?"

"Sure, but most people haven't even read *Moby-Dick*."

"Eh. I like stories about noble beasts—whales are cool, but I prefer dinosaurs."

This was eight months ago in a bar called Bangarang. The bar was in an old warehouse of uncertain purpose; they all were, these new watering holes, all in reappropriated places of obsolete labor. How quaint it all looked now, the spine of an ancient hydraulic lift decorating the entranceway, the bar itself seemingly constructed from the left-behind assembly line.

They'd both puzzled over the list of signature cocktails and discussed the strange obligation they felt to try something new in a place like this, to find out what the "soupcon of sriracha" was like in the mezcal-based drink called the Che Guava-ra, which from the description did not seem to have any actual guava. They both just wanted beer, though, and were slightly troubled by the sight of the bartender pouring cocktails not from a stainless steel shaker but from a glass laboratory beaker.

"Is that a real beaker?" Vlad asked, and the bartender scoffed.

"Why would I get a fake beaker? This is the real thing, borosilicate glass. Resistant to both thermal stress *and* shock."

Which is what got Vee onto the subject of Berkelium, and here they were, now on their third round of pints.

"Yeah, I dig dinos too," Vlad said. "My favorite? T-Rex.

When I was a kid, I tried to climb the T-Rex skeleton at the Natural History Museum. Made it almost to his ribcage before security pulled me off." He scratched his nose in a circumambulating way that suggested he desperately needed to pick it but wanted to be polite. "Even cracked the T-Rex's leg bone. What is that, like the tibia? Femur? I mean, I didn't crack it. I was a kid, light, and a really good climber. I could climb anything. So, you know, I could easily scale a skeleton without doing damage. No, it was the security guard who broke the femur." Scratched his nose again, such restraint. "My mom still had to pay for it, though. Bullshit. Whole thing got written up in the *Chronicle*. Still got the clipping, if you ever wanna see it."

"Is that like a male-female thing?"

"Everything is."

"No, I just mean the female likes dinosaurs so she looks and observes. The male likes dinosaurs so he mounts and climbs, tries to win it."

She worried that this sounded more critical than she wanted, so she touched his knee.

"What can I say, I'm just a good climber. Still am. I can climb anything, like a monkey. I could climb that thing over there," pointing a tattooed hand to the hydraulic lift. "Just ask me and I'll do it."

She tore off and rolled between her fingers a corner of her damp cocktail napkin, delicate as cotton candy. "I'll tell you what I'll ask you to do."

"Anything. Wanna see me climb the traffic light outside?"

"I want you to crash a party with me."

Technically, it wasn't crashing, Vee realized. Pam had sent her an invitation to her and Geoff's Christmas party, a.k.a. the Snowflake Soiree, but it seemed like Pam had gone out of her way to make Vee feel like an afterthought. The invitation arrived in the form of a forwarded email only two days before. It seemed like Pam had emailed all her friends, then, weeks later, remembered Vee.

Vee arrived at the party with Vlad a little drunk. Pam greeted her with smiley admonishment for not wearing an ugly Christmas sweater. "We're having a contest!"

Vee planted Vlad down at a card table amidst the bustle of red and green sweaters with boxy Santas and Rudolphs, and they drank ladled mugfuls of spiced rum cider. The more they drank, the more wildly Vlad gesticulated and the more the partiers seemed uncomfortable in his immediate vicinity, so she kept ladling more seasonal hooch into his Mrs. Claus mug.

A while later, while some busty blond was being awarded ugliest sweater for a tannenbaum number festooned with fuzzy balls, Vlad and Vee escaped the little award ceremony and ensuing "Chinese" gift exchange, and found the guestroom where they made out on the foam futon. Vlad's scruff hurt a little but she liked it, and there was a consumptive quality to his kissing, an almost teenage enthusiasm. Indeed, there was an exhilarating adolescent thrill to the whole endeavor, drunkenly hooking up in a room of someone else's house, a party murmuring outside.

Vlad looked at her, tried to focus a moment, said, "Your teeth are so sexy." Vee ran her tongue over her front teeth, feeling where the right had snuck over the left. His breath was lightly structured with cinnamon and he kissed her nose a couple times, actually submerged her whole proboscis in his mouth.

A bit later, they were quietly fucking. Because he

39

thought her teeth were sexy. Because he'd been wearing an undershirt that said WORLD'S BEST MOM. Because of his accordion language, blowing extra syllables into short words and compressing longer words. Because she wanted to.

But instead of fully enjoying it, she found her mind drifting. A joke she'd heard once: Queen Victoria's advice to her daughter on her wedding night: *Just lie back and think of England.* And Vee had to hold back laughter, not at Vlad—who was thrusting with strange yogic movements, his face buried in the scoop of her neck—but at her own inability to enjoy the present-tense action. She'd recently begun to feel like she wasn't herself, but rather the sportscaster to herself, living entirely in the removed commentary. Focus, focus. The hand supporting her ass, the mouth now on her ear. Focus.

Then, just as she was returning to her body, to the activity at hand, someone opened the door. A reflex, an old habit from kidhood—she closed her eyes and went limp, feigning sleep: if I can't see you, you can't see me. While Vlad, apparently unaware, continued. When she heard the door close a few seconds later, she opened her eyes. The intruder had left. She ran her hand up the back of Vlad's neck and through his hair. He was shuddering toward completion.

Three.

She has the present. She just needs Charlie.

But Waylon had the right idea. This thing is too hot now. If Pam sees her with this—hellfire. Best to stash it somewhere. Not back in the raspberries, but somewhere only she can find it.

The tree-house isn't too far from here. She thinks. Down this path, between those garden beds filled with elderberry bushes with their fruit hanging in clumps like hornets nests. On her way, just as she passes bunchings of bok choy, she practically trips over that girl, the one with the French braid, who's lying in the dirt path with her hand raised flat about six inches from the ground.

"What'cha got there, kid?"

"This worm is crossing the street and the sun was in his eyes so I'm helping him."

True, the sun, getting lower, is now at that fierce angle that seems determined to blind you. And this worm here is inching right toward it. Vee squats, sets the present down.

"So what's your name?"

The girl looks up, squints as if deciding if Vee is worthy of this information. "Celia."

"I'm Vee. Celia, remember when you said you'd find Charlie for me?"

Celia returns to her mission of worm-centric altruism.

"Did you know that that worm there is both a boy and a girl?" Vee says, hearing herself slip back into her kid-tone. "Isn't that crazy?"

Celia looks at Vee. "I already know that stuff. My mom made me take an LGBT-tolerance class." She returns to her mission.

"Oh," Vee says. "That's nice."

"She made me because I called my teacher a faggot."

"Jesus," Vee says, or thinks she says. "You're quite the—little sparkplug, huh?"

"The Briggs-Meyer says I'm an ESTP. My mom says that means I'm a giver."

"Well, listen, ESTP, did you ever find him? Did you ever find Charlie?"

"Of course. I said I would."

"Then I need you to find him again for me."

The worm is noodling around an upshoot of some errant sprig.

"I need you to find him for me and bring him to the tree-house."

Celia looks up. She has a downward, centimeter-long scar above her left eye, some bits of dirt on the side of her face where she was resting on the ground. She turns back to the worm. "My mom says I'm not allowed to go up in the tree-house because Charlie's mom says it's dangerous."

"Why did she say it's dangerous?"

"Nails. You could step on one. Tetanus. Lockjaw."

"Well, you should tell your mom to tell Charlie's mom that the person who very lovingly made the tree-house used screws, not nails."

"Oh."

"But you don't have to go up in the tree-house. Just bring Charlie *to* the tree-house. Okay?"

"Maybe. As an ESTP, I'm a good negotiator."

"Just bring the birthday boy to the tree-house."

At the tree-house, Vee looks around for adults. None in

the vicinity that she can see, though she can hear a low-frequency conversation grumbling around somewhere, maybe through those dragon fruit plants. She'll have to be careful. She wants to stash the present up in the tree-house; the single platform of its construction would perfectly hide it from view. But she realizes now that she can't hold the present and climb the tree at the same time. For a ladder she screwed thick, foot-long sections of wood into the trunk, and their once-crisp and yellow lumber flesh-tone has since weathered to match the gray of the tree's bark, as if the tree has successfully taken the graft, incorporated the alien wood as its own.

She starts poking around for something she can stand on when she finds another kid. It's the boy she saw when she first got here, the one fiercely tugging on his pecker, and now here he is again, hiding in the foliage, busying his hands. He looks up, still sucking on his lower lip, seems quiet enough and focused more on bodily pleasures than material ones, that she could use him to stash the present and he wouldn't snitch or steal.

"Hey," she says. "Wanna be useful?"

He shakes his head.

"Well, come here anyway."

She guides him, hand on his bony back, to the base of the tree. She kneels down to face him, her thighs starting to ache from all this crouching down to kid-level. "What's your name?"

"Owen," he whispers.

"Listen, Owen the Onanist, here's what you're going to do. You're going to climb up to that tree-house up there, and I'm going to hand you this present. Think you can do that?"

He looks up at the tree-house. His voice helium-drunk, he says, "What about the rusty nails?"

"Oh, for Christ's sake—" Vee breathes deeply. "There are no fucking nails sticking out. How incompetent do you think I am?"

He shrugs.

"Okay, just scoot up there and I'll hand you the present. Then scoot back down, real quick-like."

She stands back up, and he tentatively grabs the footholds. He's not the most confident climber, doesn't seem to trust his own feet. If only Vlad were here. Vlad: she's never met a man more in his own body. To be a dude, it seems, is to never question your ownership and manipulation of your body.

Owen is near the top now and wedges himself in the crotch of the tree just below the floor of the tree-house.

"Here," she says, lifting up the present, handing it to him. "Can you toss it onto the tree-house there?"

He looks for a moment like he's going to just stay up in the tree and horde the present for himself.

"Just put it on those boards there."

He finally complies. Sure enough, the tree-house perfectly hides the present from view.

"Aren't tree-houses supposed to have walls?"

"Okay, kid, come down."

"It's just a floor."

"How many houses you built, huh?"

"And it's all slanty."

"You need to come down now." Vee reaches up to him. "Come on."

He turns his butt out to descend, his right foot searching blindly for a footing below him.

"Careful, kid."

He pulls his foot back into the crotch of the tree. "I can't."

"Just come down, same way you went up, just in reverse."

"I'm stuck."

"No, you're not."

She climbs up the first two rungs of the ladder, high enough to easily grab his foot.

"What are you *doing*?" There's a clear tone of terror in his voice now. Next: tears, screaming, adults swarming in.

"I'm going to place your foot on the step, and you'll be able to climb down from there." She does, but he still doesn't move.

Some rustling nearby. Could just be one of the chickens, hopefully. But the sound is coming closer and has a definite human-footstep pace and rhythm.

"Owen, you need to come down immediately, do you understand?"

"I can't!"

Footsteps getting closer, she pulls on his ankle. "I got you, just climb down." She pulls on his ankle again and her own foot slips from the foothold. She instinctively holds Owen's ankle tighter to save herself and, as she falls, pulls Owen down with her. She lands back flat on the dirt and the kid lands elbows out on her stomach. The wind knocked out of her, she can't ask Owen if he's okay, so she just holds him a moment. He looks up at her, too traumatized to speak, much less scream or cry.

The footsteps are here now, and Vee closes her eyes, rests her head on the ground, tries to resign herself to the inevitable scolding from some parent.

"Aunt Colleen!"

She opens her eyes. It's Charlie. Standing above her.

Owen scrambles off her, stepping on her boob in the process, and runs away.

"Charlie!" She pulls herself to her knees, where she's about his height, and gives him a hug. "You're so big!"

Celia is standing behind him a few yards.

"So are you," Charlie says.

She tries to remember the last time she saw him. By the time she and Vlad arrived at the Christmas party, Charlie had gone to bed. Before that, then. Maybe his birthday last year, the one at the bowling alley.

Celia, looking fidgety from neglect, runs away.

"So observant," she says.

Charlie's hair, blindingly blonde last year, is now darker, rusty. Still cut in a utilitarian moptop, though. And his face is a little leaner, like he's finally emerged from the anonymity of toddler-chub, becoming determinedly identifiable—in the pinched bridge of his nose, the astringent mouth—as Pam's son. Except that he's wearing sweatpants. Pam has never worn sweatpants. She once said sweatpants represent everything that's wrong with America. Charlie must have put up an admirable fight to get into these.

"Aunt Colleen," he says. "Mommy said you weren't coming."

"Yes, well. I'm not actually Colleen anymore."

Charlie blinks a few times. "You're not Colleen?"

"Not anymore."

"Who are you?"

"I mean, I'm still me. Kind of. But my name is now Vee."

"Why?"

46

There are rivulets of clear snot on Charlie's upper lip. She covers her hand with her sleeve and wipes his face. Charlie, surely used to this sort of thing, remains perfectly passive. But now he has black soot on his lip. Vee looks at her sleeve, realizes she used it earlier to clean out her pipe before giving it to Waylon. She takes her other sleeve and wipes away the soot.

"I take it back," she says. "I like your first question. If I'm no longer Colleen, then who am I? I'm Vee now. And I'm Vee because I no longer wanted to be Colleen."

"Why?"

"You see, Colleen was... well, she wasn't me. So my old man and I, we went to the courthouse in Seattle—"

"Why?" he interrupts. Vee was trying to build suspense and profundity by offering some contemplative and dramatic pauses, and he just blitzed right in. She's got to keep a strong and steady momentum if she's gonna get through any story with this kid.

"It's complicated," she says. "That's just how you do it. But the point is we changed our names. And I became Vee. And so now I'm Vee."

"You can change your name?"

"Yup."

"Can you change your name to *anything*?"

"I know a guy who changed his name to Anaconda. He—" She stops herself, in part because Charlie is now laughing in conniptions, and in part because she realizes that explaining the name's origin might not be appropriate.

"Hey," she says, touching his shoulder as his giggles dissipate. "Want a surprise?"

"Mommy asked me that and she took me to the dentist."

47

"Well, this is not the dentist. This is something better. This is a—" She mouths the word *present* and then puts her finger over lips, *shush*.

Charlie's eyes widen. He nods.

She smiles, raises her eyebrows conspiratorially. Or at least she hopes it comes across that way. She knows she's not very good at controlling them as tools of expression, worries her eyebrow bounce looked more like a seizure. If it did, Charlie doesn't care. He's got a birthday present on the mind.

She points up at the tree-house and he asks, "It's up there?"

She nods. "Uh-huh."

"But Mommy said no gifts."

"Yes, Charlie, I'm now aware of that, thank you."

"But you brought one?"

"I did."

"For me? But Mommy said—"

"Charlie," Vee says. "Let's play a game. Every time you want to say 'Mommy,' instead say 'Cloaca.'"

"Clo—" He's watching her mouth.

"Clo-a-ca."

"That's a funny name."

"It's—" She's about to tell him the truth, that it's the term for an animal's orifice that serves urinary, intestinal, and reproductive purposes, a disgustingly messy all-purpose hole, but stops herself. "It is, isn't it. So. Your gift. Wanna go get it?"

He's staring up at the tree-house and whispers, as if to himself, "Yeah."

She can't wait for him to tear open the wrapping paper, rip open the box, and see the dinosaur, that infinitely shrunken plastic analogue of one of those massive beasts, their bodies like a single muscle, big enough to flex and feel the curve of the earth, their sheer size reminders of your own speck-like existence, the sight of one, even flayed of its flesh and hung outside a museum, capable of causing irreparable awe, that sense of something dilating in you, that sense of free fall. "Let's go get it," she says

Just as Vee stands up, a bell starts chiming, a loud metal clanging thing.

Charlie's distracted now, is staring in the direction of the house with meerkat intensity.

"What's that?" Vee asks.

The bell continues and over it Pam, sounding like a carnival barker, calls out, "Birthday cake! Birthday cake!"

And suddenly the yard comes alive with children stampeding cake-ward. First she just hears them, hears them emerging from the bushes and trees, but then she sees them, whizzing past, all limbs and craven need for sugar. Mob mentality is strong and Charlie is not immune. He runs along with them.

"Charlie!" Vee shouts. "Come back!"

But he's gone.

At the stretch of grass between the house and the microgreens, Pam and Geoff have covered a picnic bench in red-checkered paper and laid out stacks of paper plates and tubs of sporks. A *Happy Birthday* banner has been strung between trees. Pointy party hats make it look like a crowd of sharpened pencils.

By the time Vee gets there, Charlie has already taken his place at the head of the picnic table, kids crammed onto the benches as if onto life-rafts. She sees them all there:

Celia, Waylon, Declan, a fuck-ton of others, all staring at Charlie or the center of the table where they're anticipating a cake to appear. The adults are surrounding them, nursing beers and beer-bellies.

Pam emerges from the crowd holding a remarkably authentic-looking crown high into the air. It's gold, tarnished and weathered, crenelated with little fleur-de-lis and studded with emeralds. And Vee can tell from the way Pam's holding it that it has a definite heft to it.

The crowd oohs, ahs, claps.

"Attention, attention," Pam shouts, making her way closer to Charlie. "All ye gathered here today bear witness and pay tribute to the glorious birthday of one Sir Charlie Lennon Ketchum! On this day, this day of days, one-fifth-of-a-score ago, the right honorable Sir Charlie, after fourteen hours of labor that nearly destroyed his mother's tentative grip on sanity—"

The adults offer polite laughter, surely trying to forget the visceral account of the labor that Pam foisted upon any and all listeners four years ago.

Pam waits for the laugh to pass like a sitcom actor of old, and then, in an accent of vague and slippery origin, continues: "I present to you here, upon this day of celebratory celebration, this crown of gold, which I will coronate upon the pate of the young birthday gentleman, Sir Charlie!"

The crowd goes wild in its tame way. Charlie and the kids, at least, look excited. Their eyes are fixed on the crown, the goddamn crown.

Bitch has a crown.

"And so," Pam says, addressing Charlie but still in her ridiculous voice, "with the laying on your head of this coronet, I wish you a most happy birthday."

She brings the absurd thing down slowly onto smiling Charlie's head and the crowd again gives a cheer.

"Thank you, Cloaca."

The crowd offers a confused chuckle and Charlie looks around, sees Vee and smiles. Vee improvises a "no" in sign language, remembers all the kids are learning ASL these days, but realizes her own spastic attempts at it look more like she's a puppeteer without a puppet. Plus, now a suspicious- and confused-looking Pam is following Charlie's line of sight to Vee, to whom she offers a pert smile.

"And now," Pam continues, shaking it off, "Young Sir Charlie will call forth for the feast!"

Pam looks at Charlie. It's his cue apparently and he has no idea what to do.

Pam says, "Go ahead, call forth for your feast!"

Silence.

Charlie's folding under the pressure. He rubs his forehead where the crown seems to be irritating him. He shifts in his seat, slouches.

Pam whispers something to him, but he just grips his head with both hands, as if to help his neck hold up the weight of the crown.

"Did he say it?" It sounds like Geoff's voice, from behind the crowd. "I can't hear anything back here."

Pam yanks on her bangs a moment, then calls back, "He didn't say it, but just—just bring it out."

Geoff lets out a rebel yell and rushes through the crowd holding a cake on a baking sheet. People make way for him and he makes it to the table where Vee can see the cake in more detail. It's a car, a racing car of some

51

sort, all black and blue, perhaps the Batmobile, made with an intense level of detail and precision. It looks, at first glance, like an actual toy plastic car, but look closer and you can see the soft texture of the frosting lipping up around where the four candles are stuck into the roof.

The crowd begins a rendition of the "Happy Birthday" song, a melody that no matter how energetically performed always sounds like it's sung by prisoners on a death march, and the moment it ends, Floyd, videotaping the whole thing on some teensy device, says, "Can we do that again with a non-copyrighted song so I can post the video online?"

A few laugh and Floyd says, "Come on, I'm serious."

People start chanting for Charlie to blow out his candles. Charlie's definitely looking less enthusiastic now. He's stooped pretty low, his eyes squinting. The crowd continues to implore him to blow out the candles. He lifts his head for the task and leans forward, and that's when he collapses. Heavy from the crown, his head the anchor, he falls, right off the chair and onto the ground.

The parents rush in, swarm the downed child. Vee can't see but is acutely aware that she's the only adult not actively engaged in a performance of concern. Even Floyd is hovering over the scene with his palm-device camera. Documenting perhaps with Internet-virality in mind. Vee stays put, just watches kids toggle between fear and hilarity, unsure.

Sure enough, someone, one of the dads, shouts, in what might be a *Wayne's World* allusion, "And he's okay!" and Geoff lifts Charlie, who's looking slightly dazed, up onto his shoulders, and everyone cheers.

Pam picks the crown up off the ground, flicks dirt off, and places the thing carefully on the table beside the cake.

"Okay, champ," Geoff says, "wanna take another shot at the cake?"

Charlie bops his father's head like an ineffectual bongo player and says, "No."

Geoff lifts Charlie off his shoulders and sets him standing on the table. "Come on, Charlie, give those candles a good blow."

"No."

A nervous hush, people anticipating a tantrum.

"I don't want to be Charlie anymore."

Vee sees where this is going, tenses.

"I'm changing my name to Batman!"

People laugh, some kids too, but there's still a nervous energy shot through the adults' reactions. Everyone, it seems, can hear the tone of entitlement in the birthday boy's voice, and Pam and Geoff here are on stage, surely scrutinized for how they're going to handle the situation.

"Well," Geoff says, "Batman is a creature of night, so I don't think he'd be too crazy about that candlelight there threatening his cover of darkness. Best to blow it out."

Good, sweet Geoff, he of the inexhaustible collection of puffy-crotched khakis, he of the froggy double chin that's totally incongruous with his slight frame, that chin that always seems to mark him as an inevitable cuckold when standing beside the razored beauty of Pam. When Vee first met Geoff, she never thought it would work out, thought Pam would trample this quiet, hunched man, and Vee hoped that one day this guy would find some lady who'd find that ridiculous chin to be the sexiest goddamn wattle ever. Maybe that's Pam, after all, maybe she gropes its softness like it's a tit, creams herself.

Charlie says, "I need to go to the courthouse in Seattle

and change my name to Batman. That's how you do it."

Most people seem to ignore this comment, but Pam, all-knowing Pam, is laser-cutting targets in Vee's forehead with those eyes of hers.

"Come on, champ," Geoff says. "One good huff and puff and those candles'll be out."

But it doesn't work. Charlie-cum-Batman has lost interest in cake, isn't even looking at it. He raises his hands above his head, lets them collapse back down, done. "Hide and seek! I want to play hide and seek!"

Pam and Geoff appear to have some sort of silent conversation entirely with their eyebrows, and then, with a swiftness that suggests these two know what happens when Charlie's hide and seek demands are not met, Pam shouts, in that voice again, "Hear ye, hear ye! According to ancient tradition, the cake ceremony will commence only after the traditional round of Hideth and Seeketh! The birthday boy will hide and only when we, his subjects, find him will he cut for us the communion!"

Pam's shtick is certainly appropriating an increasingly diverse and disturbing range of rhetoric. Apparently now the cake is the body of Christ? "Jesus," Vee mumbles.

But Pam acts quickly in herding the group into game mode while Geoff whisks the cake away from salivating kids.

In no time the whole cast of partiers, adults and kids, are all lined up facing the house, and Pam announces the rules: that everyone will remain facing the house with their eyes closed for the duration of her count to thirty, during which time Charlie will hide anywhere on the property.

Vee is standing between Celia and that guy Ryan,

staring at cracked gray stucco while her older sister counts down: "Twenty-one. Twenty. Nineteen."

Ryan nudges Vee, smiles at her. "You gotta close your eyes," he says out of the corner of his mustachioed mouth, his soul-patch like a diacritical mark that adds a predatory lilt to all his words.

She crosses her arms, closes her eyes.

"Fifteen. Fourteen. Thirteen."

She can sense Ryan leaning over to her, smell his pomade. He whispers, "I think I need to talk to you about something."

He probably wants to come out to her as a fat fetishist, be rewarded for his bravery with a blowjob. She holds her breath, inches slightly away from him, toward Celia.

"Nine. Eight. Seven."

She turns away from Ryan, away from the house, and opens her eyes a crack: Charlie disappearing down the path toward the tree-house.

"Ah, ah, ah," Ryan whispers. "No cheating."

"Five. Four. Three."

She closes her eyes and turns back to the house. Ryan's pomade smells like some sort of factory lubricant, like a greasy orgy of mechanics, like the industrial revolution.

"One! Okay, Charlie, hope you're well hidden, because we're coming to find you!"

Everyone turns and starts walking into the garden. The kids all run, but the parents just walk, fanning out like a search party.

Vee wants to bolt to the tree-house, but she keeps the sad pace of the adults so as not to arouse suspicion. Passing the asparagus, she realizes Ryan is following her. Once in the cover of higher foliage, she picks up the pace.

"Scuse me," Ryan calls behind her. He jogs to catch up and is soon walking beside her. "First thing, if you're going to cheat at hide and seek, you have to make your seeking look a bit more natural, less like a bee-line. Second thing—"

"Not a good time for thing number two," she says, stumbling a bit on a root. "My boyfriend," she says, unsure how to finish the sentence but just wanting to throw the reference out there as a potential boner-killer. "My boyfriend, he couldn't make it today. He was busy."

"Totally," Ryan says. "I get it."

They're almost at the tree-house and Vee is contemplating an elaborate maneuver to lose this guy, but in trying to formulate the specifics of how a maneuver like that might actually work, all she can think of are those scenes in movies when the protagonist gets into a cab, says, "I'm being followed, can you lose him?" and the tactful cabbie swerves his magic through New York streets.

And now, here they are: at the base of the tree-house, Ryan still beside her. This guy's like a social disease; you surely need some prescription shampoo to properly rid yourself of him.

She can't see anything or anyone in the tree-house, but if Charlie is huddled down at all there's no way anyone would be able to see him from the ground.

"Charlie!" she shouts. "I mean—Batman!"

The sound starts like a heartbeat, suddenly louder and faster and beating with a physical force against her chest and she wonders if this is what a heart attack feels like, but then she realizes the sound is outside of her body, the rhythm pounding at her with the air as its weapon, and she looks up and sees the belly of a helicopter—black on white letters reading *POLICE*—barnstorming the backyard, swooping by, barely clearing the trees. In a second it's out of sight, but the sheer force of that sound remains, throbbing in the air. Even the silence it leaves in its wake rings wounded in her ears, but she can hear kids screaming, crying. Ryan has run off, apparently, and adults are shouting to come back to the house, come back, olly olly oxen free!

Around her, a few kids scurry by, just as galvanized as when they stampeded for cake. Fear and hunger seem indistinguishable in the actions of children, their proximity to the primordial soup of their in-vitro existence meaning their bodies know more than hers the primal sameness of all self-preserving expressions. Come to think of it, that's why she likes getting high, drunk, what-have-you ("what-have-you" being a favorite expression of Vlad's, just because he always follows it with, "No, seriously, what have you got? I'm looking for some"). When intoxicated the barrier between emotion and sensation reveals itself as porous at best, everything simply an expression of some vital urge. Laugh, cry, fuck.

"Olly, olly, oxen free!"

She wishes Vlad were here. Or some version of him.

A few more kids run by.

She looks up to the tree-house.

"Charlie? Batman, are you up there?"

Floyd jogs by on his way to the house. He grabs her by the shoulder, to get moving, and says, "Come on, come on. No dawdling. Didn't you see that thing? The fucking rioters are headed this way!"

Protesters renamed rioters, Charlie becoming Batman,

Pam renamed Cloaca, Colleen becoming Vee. Guess it's all a matter of who's doing the naming. Who gets to sit at the grown-up table, who gets to speak.

Even Vlad started as someone else. Born Stuart Murphy. She still has trouble believing it. She only discovered it three months ago when she went with him to sign the lease on the warehouse in West Oakland where they've since been living. There it was, written on the lease in his wobbly cursive, Stuart Murphy.

"Who the fuck is that?" she said.

"No one," he said.

"No one? Is that *you?*"

"Stuart Murphy was a friendless fuck who shit his pants in algebra. I'm Vlad."

"Please, everyone does that stuff when they're kids."

"This was at City College. I'm Vlad."

They were standing in the two-thousand square foot space, empty and cavernous, cement floor splattered with paint from the artists' collective that used to occupy it. The manager, a paraplegic guy whose wheelchair was tricked out with Christmas lights, was zooming out to his van to get the key to the warehouse's ten-by-fifteen storage unit, where Vee and Vlad would eventually set up their bedroom, leaving the warehouse space itself for the twelve long rows of marijuana plants, in garden beds propped on folding tables, garden beds she and Vlad had to make themselves that looked frustratingly like those in Pam and Geoff's yard.

"I'm not a gardener," she'd told Vlad when he'd first told her his dream of opening a pot farm and dispensary, call it Vlad the Inhaler's. Vee had spent one season trimming up in Humboldt, but her skills never went beyond rote muscle memory.

"It's not gardening," he'd said. "It's science."

But in that moment, there in the empty warehouse, the sunlight finding every hole in the roof and coming down in spears, the freeway outside wheezing away, she felt this new knowledge of his name dilate something inside her, the negative space of all the other things she didn't know about him. Vertiginous, looking at him, suddenly seeing all that she couldn't see.

By the time they got their stuff moved in and spent their first night in the warehouse, mattress flopped down on cement, amidst haphazardly packed boxes (Vee's stuff) and haphazardly packed Hefty bags (Vlad's stuff), this new awareness was becoming a source of quiet panic.

The past few weeks, Vlad the Inhaler's had been inching, with stoned alacrity, toward actualization. Vlad said he knew a graphic designer who could modify that famous portrait of Vlad the Impaler with some cannabis iconography. Vlad was investing in UV lights, variously sized glassine baggies. He spent a lot of time looking at websites that allowed you to design your own business card, indecisive, mumbling about brand identity, the debilitating variety of possibilities.

And here she was, staring in the blue darkness, at Vlad lying beside her, the debilitating variety of possibilities that was Vlad.

Confirmable results. Verifiable facts. That's what she needed. But with each new mystery, the endlessly branching network of possibility, she felt him slipping further and further away, Stuart Murphy becoming a blurry abstraction. Like reading a *Choose Your Own Adventure* novel, getting to the end and realizing that this ending was not really *the* ending, just *an* ending, one determined entirely by the biases of the observer, bad science. How much had she formulated Vlad from her own propensities and tilts? One thing about those *Choose Your Own Adventure* novels, you could always go back, suss out where you went wrong. Countless branchings of possibility didn't necessarily mean nothing was certain—it just meant you had to be more interrogative in establishing certainty, more determined to lock down clear answers.

Vlad was on his back, his face in profile, his Adam's apple a visual echo of his jutting nose. He always sleeps slab-flat on his back as if on display at a wake. She leaned over and kissed him. Being pulled gently into sleep, he kissed her back with a lazy delay. His lips still had the tang of her cunt. His nose whistled slightly with his breath.

She shook him. He startled awake. He mumbled some syllables of uncertain intent.

"Vlad," she said.

"Huh?"

"Will you marry me?"

Four.

Back at the picnic tables, the adults have gathered like circled wagons.

Floyd's wife is the only outlier, tending to the kids over at the picnic table. She's slicing up the cake for them, keeping them distracted with sugar. "But we can't have cake yet," says Owen. "We didn't find Charlie!" And Waylon thwacks him on the arm.

Geoff seems to be missing from the adult crowd, but everyone else is here. Pam, thumbing her cell phone, is tensed like a tightrope. "My data might be incomplete. I have the rioters positioned last at San Pablo and University. They shut down the intersection, broke some windows. Tear-gas, looks like. Police firing rubber rounds."

The peanut gallery speaks:

"That's miles from here. Two at least."

"They can't move *that* fast."

"Then what *was* that? That," whispering, "ghetto bird?"

"Maybe it just lost its homing device, didn't realize it wasn't in the ghetto anymore."

"They must be here, the rioters, out in the streets. Here! They must!"

"Should we send someone outside to see if they see anything?"

"Christ. We didn't board up our windows or anything."

"I can't believe this. I mean, sure—injustices, I get it. But *this*? How're we to get home? If they're shutting down the streets?"

"We shouldn't leave tonight." This from Floyd, sounding serious, militantly focused. "It's only going to get worse when the sun goes down. That's how it works. Maybe Pam's intel is old, but if they're at San Pablo and University, that means they have easy freeway access. If they get onto the freeway and shut it down? Think about that. Driving home, we'll all get caught. Do you want your kids to be sitting there, fish in a barrel, for the rioters?"

"He's right. Pam, what's your guest room situation?"

Ryan catches Vee's eye. He seems to have a non-parent detachment from this all.

"Okay," Pam says, relaying from her phone, "okay, okay. Listen, listen. Reports of protesters at Shattuck and Cedar. Just a few, but—hoodies. *Black* hoodies."

The bearded gentleman says, "I just don't know how a so-called liberal could wear black, like they know nothing about the history of fascism. I mean—"

"That's point-six miles away," Pam says. "They can't— they can't—they have no right to do this. Not here, not in *my* city."

"Shattuck and Cedar? That's the gourmet ghetto. Chez Panisse. We have reservations tomorrow. *Down*stairs."

"They can't do this!" Pam shouts, finally looking up from her phone. "They can't destroy my city. These people, these *thugs*."

"Oh, man," Vee says, louder than she intends. "You're just dying to drop a few n-bombs, aren't you, sis?"

"Excuse me?" Pam directs all energies right at Vee, and the peanut gallery turns accordingly. "*Excuse* me? How dare you. How *dare* you. That's *not* what I meant. I went to Berkeley, for Christ's sake." She's now waving her cell phone at Vee. "You can't launch an accusation like that at me—I went to Berkeley!"

Pam's favorite card to play, the Cal card. But of course, as Pam scolded her once, you don't call it *Cal*, not unless you're at a football game, that's just gauche—it's *Berkeley*, as if the institution absorbed the city, the institution where Free Speech was once a movement but is now just the name of a café that sells ten-dollar Pop Tarts to undergrads paying Stanford-level tuition. Of course, Pam's real agenda is to remind Vee that Vee herself didn't get in.

"Yeah," Vee says, "Berkeley, lots of black people there. Who else is gonna empty your trash?"

"She's just drunk." This from Floyd's wife, having returned from kid-tending. "Look at her. Don't worry about her, Pam."

"I minored in conflict and peace studies," Pam says. "I get it. I put my body upon the gears, the whole fucking deal."

"Pam, please," another adult says. "Language. The kids."

"But this," Pam says, "this isn't that. This is just—this is chaos! I have every right to be angry. I voted for Obama!"

Vee feels eyes on her like salt on a slug.

"It's easy to be snarky when you don't care about anything." Pam's calming herself now, staring Vee down. "If you ever have kids, if you ever care enough to protect someone other than yourself, then you can talk."

Geoff runs up, his pate glistening with sweat. "I can't find Charlie. Did anyone see where he ran to?"

Pam snaps to. As swiftly as she redirected her outrage at the protesters to outrage at Vee, she now redirects that energy to the Charlie hunt, and without a word she speed-walks off into the garden.

With Pam gone, all eyes shift to Vee. Or at least she thinks they do. At the moment, she's examining the still life of a well-wormed crabapple at her feet. She's not good with outbursts. She always wants the pure catharsis of a good bout of righteous anger but whenever she comes close to one—even a tentative step toward one, like a sarcastic barb at her older sister—she inevitably suffers the hangover of embarrassment. Own it, Vlad would say—no apologies. That's his refrain, always applicable. Always.

She turns and, ignoring the peanut gallery, walks off into the cabbage and radicchio. She keeps going until she finds coverage behind the fruit trees, moving toward the chicken coop.

Before she can make it to the coop, she hears footsteps behind her again, hustling to catch up with her.

She stops and turns, sees Ryan.

"Jesus fucking Christ."

"I like what you said back there."

She shouts: "Just leave me the fuck alone, okay?"

Here it is, perhaps, the unapologetic catharsis she wants. Maybe the trick is to just direct it at someone lower on the hierarchy. And guys with stupid facial hair are always lower on the hierarchy than her. As a matter of policy. She continues: "Just fuck right off. I'm not gonna suck your dick, all right?"

Ryan's moustache twitches shock. "What?"

Clearly mistaken about his intentions, she braces herself for the first wave of post-outburst shame.

"I just need to talk to you." He steps closer. "I remembered where I recognized you from."

"The Internet," she says, keeping up her furious tone in a nod to Vlad's wisdom. "Who cares?"

"You were at the Christmas party." He's scrunching his eyebrows in a forced display of sincerity. "Back in

December."

"Yes, thank you for that clarification. I'm never quite sure what month people have Christmas parties."

"I was looking for the bathroom," he says, "and I opened the wrong door."

She tries to push past him, but he doesn't move— "Listen," he says—so she has to trample the posies to get by him and speedwalk with Pam-like elbow-thrusting away from the coop, up to the clearing with the beer cooler.

"Listen," he says, already on her tail. "I saw that guy, that guy you came with. Listen, you were passed out and he—listen to me! I'm speaking to you!"

He's right at her shoulder now. She turns and shoves him back. Stumbling, recovering, he says, "Listen."

"Just shut the fuck up!"

"No! I'm a good guy here. I'm doing the right thing and you're going to listen to me. I felt like an asshole when I didn't say anything before, and I'm not gonna feel like a jerk again because I'm a good fucking guy."

She tries to push him again and he grabs her by the shoulders, squeezes. His thumbs into her biceps, it hurts.

"It's none of your business," she says.

"Are you going to listen?"

She squirms, twists, tries to make knee-testicle contact, but he's got her off balance so when she lifts her knee to properly groin him, she just falls backward, pulling him with her. He lands on the ground beside her, arm momentarily draped across her breasts.

"Naughty, naughty, naughty!" It's Celia, suddenly standing beside them. Terrifying, the way kids can just apparition like this.

Celia is giggling, pointing at them.

Ryan struggles to get back up as quickly as he can, while Vee just wants to lie here a moment, in the dirt. Why not, it's where she keep landing, might as well just stay down here.

But then she sees Ryan looking like he's about to launch into his spiel again. Vee must act quickly.

Celia is still lost in her laughter, so Vee gets on her knees, turns away from Ryan, and gives all her attention and more to Celia. "You're quite the giggle monster, aren't you?" she says, tickling the kid's belly.

After a minute of Vee stoking as much hysterics from this girl as she can, Ryan—sad, ignored Ryan—walks off.

But now Vee has this maniacally laughing and convulsing creature on her hands and, now that it has served its purpose, she has no idea how to stop it. It's not as straight-forward as ministering to tears where you just counter bad with good, assurances of wonderfulness and safety. Quieting laughter, there's no way to do it without being a scrooge.

She puts her hands on Celia's shoulders, gently but firmly, and coos soothing sounds at her. Why not treat laughter and tears as the same thing; they surely are.

"What were you guys doing?" Celia asks.

"Nothing. Nothing at all. He was being mean with me so I tried to kick him in the balls."

Celia's eyes widen like they might fall out of her head. "You're never supposed to do that. That's what my daddy said."

"Well, if a guy's ever rough with you, then you're allowed."

Celia sighs as if it's her last breath. "Can I have my reward now?"

"Your reward?"

"I found Charlie for you. You said I could have the reward."

Vee exhales, scratches her ear. She fumbles in her pocket, remembers. "That boy. Waylon. He has it at the moment. Go ask him to share it with you."

Up at the beer cooler, free of Ryan, free of Celia, Vee can breathe a moment. The sun is falling, slow-motion splashing oranges and purples back up into the sky. She runs her hand through her hair, finds sticks, ambiguous bits of earth.

Opening another bottle, she wonders what her beer credit is against her gift debit.

She can see the top of the tree that has the tree-house, and perhaps has Charlie, and perhaps Charlie now has the present. She needs to get to him, properly *give* him the gift, tell him about it, forge the connections that are a given for Pam—those signals in their DNA that scream *survival is dependent on our mutual love*—but for which Vee has to work, work hard. While everyone else rests on the privilege of instinct and all it's coded to do, Vee, as she's only recently learned, has to do it all her own damn self.

The horizon is a layer of backyard forestry laid out below the bar-graph juttings of downtown office buildings silhouetted against the sunset. The men in those buildings, with their acutely angled suits and imperial view of the world below, to them it all must look like a game of Pac-Man, grids of orderly space, people—so blurry from above they're just abstract entities—moving through, gobbling each other up. But down here, she can see no grids, no order. Although she thought the tree-house on one end and the chicken coop on the other marked points of the yard's perimeter, she can't really see any fence or clear marker of property lines, as if all sense and sign of boundary, of containment, is slipping away.

The beer is giving her a slight chill. She wishes she had something warm. Whiskey, a hit, a simple sweatshirt. She spent most of her life in big, body-obscuring sweatshirts, trying to carry the pajama aesthetic of dorm attire—and its cozy anonymity—as far beyond her curtailed college career as she could. When her old roommate asked her not to accompany her to a bar because, she said, "You don't look like Colleen—you look like a sack of Colleen," she tried to ditch the sweatshirts. She even went so far as to dabble in a rockabilly look, having always admired how all these chubby rockabilly girls could, with tight cuffed Levis and a bandana or two, make their curves look like ferocious acts of intent. Though that look ultimately wasn't for her—all that time getting ready, the constriction of jeans cameltoe tight, and the ubiquitous fear that her made-up eyebrows looked like Groucho's grease moustache—she did feel a slight rush of confidence in that get-up, felt like she could take it further, join a roller derby team, feel the crunch of bone against her fist. Dressed in sweatshirts—even now, dressed in an Army surplus jacket, the only gesture toward clothing that offers the vaguest form and structure that she can maintain long-term—she feared people saw her as passive: shapeless and therefore malleable. Had she worn her old rockabilly gear today, that guy Ryan never would have laid one moustache-twirling finger on her, never would have presumed he could wrest that story away from her, rewrite it to satisfy his good-man narrative. It's her goddamn memory.

"There you are." It's Geoff, walking up to the beer cooler. He seems a little winded, perhaps still from his earlier Charlie-search.

"Here I am," Vee says.

Geoff rests one Hush Puppy on the cooler, leans his elbows on his knee, khakis freshly hashtagged with grass-stains. "How are you?"

"What?"

"I mean—" He stands up straight. "I feel like whenever we see you there's always a million other things going on and, well—" He eyes the beer in Vee's hand. "I think I'll grab one of those."

And he does. When he opens it, the bottle cap falls to the ground and he picks it up, places it into his pocket.

"You know, Pam and I, we throw these things because we love all the people in our lives, want to bring them together. But the irony is that we're so busy hosting it's hard to feel like we're really connecting with people. Or that's me at least." He takes a sip of beer, looks over the bottle as he swallows. "Hmm. Interesting."

Vee wraps her arms around herself, turns to a swell of kid-noise over near the coop, sees a rustle in the bushes.

"I just remembered," Geoff says. "When Pam first told me about you, she said how envious she was of you for being the black sheep, for being able to go your own way. When I met you—Thanksgiving, I think?—I said, 'So, you're the black sheep,' and—do you remember this?—you said the term came from sheep being born showing recessive traits, and I said I remembered doing those pundit squares in school, and you made so much fun of me for saying pundit instead of Punnett squares. I was pretty embarrassed, but then you made a joke about pundit squares being like *Hollywood Squares*. Do you remember?"

Vee bites some chapped skin from her lower lip. "Yeah. You were like, 'Who'd be the Paul Lynde of *Pundit Squares*?'"

"You said O'Reilly, made a joke about him being in the closet."

"So far in the closet he found Narnia."

"That was it!" Geoff gives a sort-of laugh, more a trace memory of whatever genuine laugh he gave five years ago.

Vee peels the label on her beer. "That wasn't my joke," she says. "I heard someone else say it."

"Still counts," he says. He clears his throat, looks out over the yard.

There's a single light mounted on the house, at the top of the gable, shining down over the yard. It reaches a few dozen feet into the yard, to the fruit trees. The bushes beyond are littered with scraps of light. After that, the darkening blue-green of the backyard.

"You need some more lights out here," Vee says.

"We gave the kids flashlights in their party-favor bags. We also thought things would be wrapping up by now."

"At least the chickens have light," Vee says, noticing the glow coming from the area of the coop.

"Heat lamps," he says, then, shifting tones: "Listen, I—" He waits for her to turn to him. "I was speaking with Ryan earlier. Ryan Molloy? And he—I see from your expression that he's probably already spoken with you about it. Okay. I just wanted to tell you that I can help in any way you like. That's not really the kind of case my firm handles, of course, but I know people, good people."

Vee wonders what exactly her face was doing when he said "your expression." With the mention of Ryan she felt herself shrinking in, retreating from her face—*I'm sorry, Vee's not here right now, please leave a message.* But her face has apparently betrayed her, exposed her in some way.

Geoff is holding his beer bottle with two hands, fingers laced around it as if in prayer.

"It's none of your business," she says.

"They're good people," he says, "good listeners."

Vee's fingers search her pocket for her pipe, her stand-in worry stone, and finds only dirt-lined seams.

Suddenly, there's another kid-scream, another emergency. Out there, somewhere in the yard. This one is more from the gut, less from the throat, less shrill than the last one. It's followed by some muffled adult noises of concern and rescue. Geoff looks off to where it's all coming from, maybe near the ficus. He looks back at Vee.

"I should—" He nods in the direction of the emergency. "But we'll talk, okay? Doesn't have to be today, but we'll talk."

He leaves.

Sure enough, there are heat lamps inside the chicken coop. She didn't notice before, but walking up to it, the little place glows like a cozy cabin in the woods. She peers in and sees the lamps hanging down from the rafters, stainless steel bowls with red bulbs. Assuming there's one cubby for each chicken, all but a few of them are here and accounted for. They're getting cozy, blinking, twitching, motors winding down, sinking into their own fat plumage. The vague warmth from the lamps is nice and Vee sits down in the dirt beside the coop's entranceway ramp, leans against the outside wall, pushing against the corrugated metal to massage her back muscles.

She could have told Geoff—she tried, hadn't she? Or had she hesitated, cozied herself—just for a moment—in Geoff's calming bedside manner, and by doing so tacitly endorsed Ryan's version.

She puts her elbows on her knees, covers her face. Her warm, dry palms on her eyelids, down her cheeks. Her fingernails on her forehead.

Impossible to keep the image out of her head, how Ryan must have seen her: passed out, helpless, being sleep-raped by some dude. Her own body seen from above, unconscious, limp, there for Vlad to do with whatever he wants, the scene there for Ryan to do with whatever he wants. Her self removed: a body apart. Vee as passive victim, Vee letting Geoff run with the story, not saying anything.

She digs her fingernails slowly into her forehead, tiny crescents in her skin. Teeth biting bottom lip, the warm and iron-rich seep of blood. Holding her breath, the heels of her palms on her eyelids, pushing in until purple and green bloom. She focuses on the details of the designs until she feels she can control them, make them look like the spirograph sparks and swirls of a bubble-chamber image, like on that poster she used to have above her bed, all those electrically charged particles zooming about so ecstatically they make the enclosed chamber look like the infinite expanse of space, galaxies now eddying beneath her eyelids.

She breathes.

She takes her hands away, opens her eyes. Her fingernails are dirtied with blood. She wipes her palm across her forehead, sees the smear of red across her lifeline.

She has to pee, her bladder a hot cramp at her core. She doesn't want to leave the comfort and safety of the coop, not yet. She doesn't want to venture out to discover what new sort of violence these kids have done to each other.

She grabs onto the coop's entry ramp, pulls herself up. She pulls her jacket and shirt up, holds them in her armpits. She unbuckles her belt, looks around, then unzips her pants, pulls them down. She feels the chill of the evening on her ass and gives a shiver. She's done this before, she can do it again, no problem. She learned the hard way not to squat, not with pants around your ankles, so she plants her feet in the dirt a couple feet from the coop and puts her back against the wall of the coop, the pressure keeping her body in a seated position, minus a chair. She holds the ramp beside her and relaxes. Or tries to relax. She's got pee-shyness something fierce. When in a public restroom, not to mention her sister's backyard, she has to go into a kind of self-guided meditation just to trick her bladder into giving up the goods and letting loose. She hums a single note to herself and pictures Niagara Falls. Doesn't work, though, because now she's also imagining all those daredevils who go over Niagara Falls in barrels, can't stop herself from imagining the stomach-clenching fear when the Earth drops out from beneath them. And now she's tense again and not peeing. Even in the privacy of her own bathroom she sometimes has trouble relaxing to pee if she knows someone is in earshot. Even Vlad. If he's tooling around outside the bathroom door, she'll have to turn on the sink faucet in order to open the sluices the tiniest bit. She's embarrassed to admit the problem to him, but she's pretty sure he's caught on, as a couple weeks ago, while eating her out, she said she needed to go pee before they went any further. His head shot up, eyes wide, chin glistening, and he said, "Pee on me." He lay down on the floor and waved her over. "Just squat over me and pee. Please." She hesitated, but then decided to give it a try. Hard to break Vlad's heart when he was just lying there on the floor, eyes closed, smiling, jerking off in anticipation. She squatted over him, saw his eager puppy-dog face between her knees and she tried. She wanted to. She did. She wanted nothing more than piss all over Vlad if that's what he really wanted. But it just wasn't happening. Her body had locked it down. After a minute, she said, "I'm sorry, baby," and walked to the bathroom, closed the door, and turned on the faucet full blast. Back in bed, later, post-coital, he said, "How can we be getting married next week if you're not even comfortable enough to pee on me?" He was joking, she was pretty sure, but it haunted her, this pee-comfort index of a relationship. She should be able to piss on him.

At least it has finally started to work now, as she's letting loose a timid dribble and starting to feel the pressure ease. A few warm rivulets run down the inside of her thighs, but for the most part her stance has allowed her maximum pee comfort, considering the circumstances. Her back, though, is starting to hurt, all her weight pushing her spine against the corrugated metal.

She suddenly notices Roosevelt standing across from her, watching. He struts closer, closer, as if curious about this situation, this woman hovering over a frothing puddle.

"Shoo," she says, waving him away. "Shoo."

But he's undeterred. A stream of steaming pee is heading toward him and he jabs his head at it a few times, then starts walking toward the source.

"Get away, you little McNugget."

He's right beside her now, pecking at the puddle of pee. What is it with everyone's interest in her micturition all of a sudden? Roosevelt seems to actually be drinking it now. She's just finishing up, bladder finally empty, and she's afraid that if she boosts herself out of this awkward propping she might knock Roosevelt in the face or something. So she swats at him, shoos him out of the way. But he pushes back and continues his dealings with the puddle. So she puts some more muscle into it and gives him a proper shove. It works, he runs away, but in the momentum of the shove she loses her balance and her left foot slides out and she feels herself go down and she grabs the ramp but it's too late and she lands with a muddy squish in the puddle.

She is a still, pure diamond of rage.

One week ago and one week after she failed to piss on Vlad, the two of them flew up to Seattle to change their names. Officially, legally. Now engaged, they'd submitted their wedding announcement to the *Chronicle*—so romantic, she'd said; yes and great publicity for the new business, he'd said—and were shocked when they got an email confirming that the announcement would run. "Damn," Vee said. "I thought newspapers only run wedding announcements for people with 'the third' in their names, when the mother of the bride is named Mitzy and is third generation Princeton."

Only problem was that it was the paper's policy to

only print the bride and groom's legal names. And Vlad the Inhaler never legally became Vlad the Inhaler. Legally, he was still Stuart Murphy. "I'm not fucking going in the paper as Stuart Murphy," he said. "Fuckin' Stew, fuckin' Murph. You know what they call a queef in Hawaii? They call it a 'murph.' For years people called me Murph—a Hawaiian pussy-fart. No. I'm changing my name. Legally. I don't care the cost."

He might not have cared about the impressive monetary cost, but the cost in time was an impossibility. The clerk at the Oakland courthouse explained that in order to get a legal name change, he'd have to get a judge's signature and the process usually takes six to eight weeks. Vlad was furious, fuming beneath the marble arches of bureaucracy, Vee trying to calm him with back rubs in case he started shouting in front of the armed guards. The *Chronicle* was going to run the announcement next week. If they pushed it back, they risked losing the spot. He needed to make the change now.

With a bit of Internet research, they discovered that the only state in the nation where you could get your name legally changed in twenty-four hours is Washington.

And so: here they were, two days before they planned on getting married, on a plane to Seattle, so Vlad could become Vlad.

They were cruising comfortably above a layer of cloud so flat it looked like you could step out onto it. She'd only been on a plane once before in her life, with her family fifteen years ago to an aunt's funeral in one of the Dakotas. She'd always been embarrassed by this strange deficit in her life and wanted Vlad to know but also realized that he would never ask her. He never asked her anything about her life. She wanted to feel outraged and hurt by this, but with him she never felt like he wasn't interested in her. Quite the opposite. She felt incredibly *seen* around him. It's just that he seemed to exist so entirely in the present tense that the only thing that mattered was her right now, not how she got here.

"I want to change my name too," she said.

Vlad nodded. "Right on."

"I never want to be Colleen again."

She decided that if he was going to become Vlad the Inhaler, she'd become Vee the Inhaler. Together, married, they'd become mom and pop Inhaler for Vlad the Inhaler's Dispensary, forge a new life together.

One more wrinkle though: after getting to Seattle, they took a cab to the courthouse, an H-shaped thing of retro imposition, an ambassador of a time when such places belied actual authority, and the lady at the Plexiglas window who wore something that looked like a miniature condom over her index finger, she moved paper with ease, turned pages, then pointed, prophylactically, at Vlad, and said, "Can't do nothing today. They're all at the conference."

"Who?"

"The judges. They're at the judge conference all week. You need a judge's signature and you'll have to wait till the judges come back."

But they were here now, right now, and they needed a fucking judge right fucking now, to which the lady calmly explained that if he didn't calm down right now he'd be arrested. "How can judges just not be at a courthouse?" Vlad demanded. "The inn is without an innkeeper!" Then he took Vee's arm and scooted out as fast as he could.

They stomped all throughout the city, went to a notary

public, went to two legal offices, took a stress-releasing trip to the top of the Space Needle, took in some vistas, the city and sea, before taking the elevator back down and continuing the quest at a pro bono legal firm specializing in homeless rights and being asked to leave.

While they sat on a bench at Pike Place, Vlad poring over the phone book, calling everyone listed as a judge, Vee watched the guys at the fish market tossing fresh trout. By the time Vlad managed to find a retired judge in Tacoma who insisted his signature is still valid and would be willing to put it on anything as long as they provided him with an hour at the Vancouver brothel Brandi's—a price Vlad negotiated down to a dinner at the Cheesecake Factory— Vee realized this was the first vacation she'd ever had.

They paid for the retired judge's cab ride to the courthouse and later his plate of angel hair and watched him fail to napkin off a soul-patch of Alfredo sauce, and on the flight home, now officially Vlad and Vee, soon to be officially married, she looked out the window again, saw the lacey array of cloud, and, during the jolts of turbulence, the split-second gestures toward freefall, she felt the tiny bursts of weightlessness, the little fissures in the law of gravity, bright specks of light getting through.

Vee, with leaves and hay from the coop, wiping piss-mud from her hips. Vee fearing these leaves might be of the poison oak varietal. Vee imagining her ass flaring red like a baboon's.

Holds the leaves in a blurry arbelos of light, confirms they're not leaves of three. Throws them down, zips up. Skin, cold and damp, tender to chafe against the denim.

A rustle, a hasty crepitation of shoes on dead leaves,

dirt. Ten feet away, fifteen. Just beyond this windbreaker of Vee-high bushes. More than one person.

"What? What?" Geoff, sotto voce.

"This." Pam, full volume.

"What is that?"

"What do you think it is?"

"I mean I know what it is, but—what about it? You wanna get high? We haven't smoked since the honeymoon."

Vee steadies herself, still as a scarecrow. More foliage than person. Blending in. Invisible.

"No. This is what the fight was over."

"That's why she attacked him?"

"To get this."

"That's—no. Sheila and Ronald would never have paraphernalia lying around their house. Maybe Celia brought it. Her parents—I mean, Marty went to Skidmore. And isn't Isobel from Santa Cruz? I mean—"

"Just—shut up. Listen. Waylon said Colleen gave it to him. Celia said Colleen gave it to her."

"Jesus."

"She brought this into our home—"

There's a tectonic shift somewhere in Vee's solar plexus—

"—gave drugs to our children."

—like it's no longer able to suppress a puke.

"I want her head"—Pam, voice like piano wire—"on a spike."

Five.

Her head getting cold, exposed, feeling like a licked fingertip stuck in the air to test wind direction. Standing under a tree, back against sharp bark, in a corner of the coop's clearing, just beyond the radius of the heat lamps.

She can hear footfalls moving in vectors around her, but no one yet has come down into the clearing.

If only she can get to the tree-house. If only she can get to Charlie and the gift. Then, even if she gets evicted, evicted from farm and family, at least she'll be holding on to one small scrap of something good. She'll at least know that Charlie just might remember his fourth birthday for one small kind gesture from that aunt he'll never be allowed to see again.

The tree-house is on the far end of the yard, and it sounds like there're search parties everywhere. Surely for Charlie, but also for her now.

The spike needs a head.

Right—as if Pam is some pure soul, as if her spinal cord were free of the trace glitches of drug-use. It was once Pam, after all, who asked Vee for drugs—years ago, sure, six or seven—when, returning to Pam's Telegraph Avenue studio after their dad's funeral—a cursory three-person service in the hospital's all-purpose chapel—returning so Vee could crash on Pam's floor, curling pet-like on a papasan cushion at the foot of the twin bed before driving the four hours back to her dorm the next morning for the first day of her sophomore year (or rather failing to drive back, opting instead to linger for years in the zombie exhaustion of city), it was there in Pam's studio, before lights out, that Pam asked if Vee had anything, anything at all that would quiet her brain a little and let her sleep, anything stronger than pinot and pot, and Vee pulled from her bag all that she had, a single pill she'd found in the desk drawer of a guy she'd spent one groping, slobbery night with, found and pocketed and later identified via Internet message boards as a Rohypnol, a roofie, a date-rape blackout pill, with its equations to short-circuit memory and motor-skills, and she was now splitting it with a butter knife to share with her grieving sister so they could both just turn off their brains for one night—so any claim Pam now makes for drug-free moralizing is bullshit.

A breeze veers by and in it she hears light percussive footfalls. The soft patter of kid-feet nearing. She shrinks further into the dark. The tiny figure appears, tumbling forward with haphazard gait.

The boy goes over to the coop's ramp, squints inside. He's facing away from Vee, but judging by the kid's studied tugging, this must be Owen the Onanist. Bless this boy. He seems so guided by his pleasure principle that he has no brain-space left for judgment or righteous indignation.

Vee whispers: "Hey. Owen."

He continues staring as if hypnotized into the warming glow of the chicken coop. This kid can solipsize himself like a pro, block out all the muted-trumpet babel of adult-speak.

She scans the rest of the clearing, listens. No sign of others.

She steps forward, into the light, approaches Owen. She walks right up to him, looks at the whirlpool part of hair at the center of his scalp.

"Hey, Owen." She again hears her cloying kid-tone inflate her voice like helium.

Owen turns around, unshocked by her sudden presence. He holds his pecker through his pants as if presenting it to her. Something so pure about Owen's embodiment of masculinity, the way he's stripped it down to its most essential: holding his dick, showing it to her.

"How's it going, buddy?"

He chews his lower lip.

"Have they found Charlie yet?"

He looks at her boobs, shakes his head.

She hears a search party approaching. She grabs Owen, heavier than expected, and carries him back into her private patch of darkness. The boy is compliant as a sack of flour. He rests her head on her breasts like it ain't no thang.

Three men appear beneath the bow of branches across the clearing. Floyd is with them. Another has a flashlight.

The flashlight's beam roves around the clearing. Vee clutches Owen's head against her breast: for him, comfort; for her, assurance that his mouth is covered if he peeps.

The glare of light narrowly misses them, moves on.

The men grumble, move out. The light from the flashlight throws shadows, stretches them across treetops as the men move away. She can gauge their growing distance from its angle. They seem to be moving toward the tree-house.

She sets Owen down. He nearly crumbles to the ground before his legs get the cue to be load-bearing again.

Vee holds him by the shoulders. "You up for a mission?"

He scratches at some sandy snot residue in the crescent crease of his nostril.

"It's of the utmost importance. Will you do it?" She gives him a light shoulder shake of encouragement. "Say yes."

"Yes."

"Good. Do you know how to get back to the house?"

He points.

"Good. Now I need you to run back to the house and tell everyone that you saw me leaving out the side gate. Got it?"

"But I didn't."

"Doesn't matter."

"It's a lie."

"It's a story."

"But—"

"You like stories?"

He nods. "Miranda the Panda."

"What's that?"

"Miranda the Panda lives in the Zoo, Miranda the Panda plays the kazoo."

"Good. Okay. Now go and tell the one about seeing me leave through the side gate." She turns him away, shoos him—"Run, run"—and he's off.

Venturing out of the coop's clearing, away from its light. Like wandering to the bathroom in the middle of the night, feeling for familiar markers, uncoordinated in half-sleep. Stepping high to avoid being got by a root again. Hands out, Helen Keller. The sounds of her footfalls now sonar. Though the foliage around her has gone dark, the sky above retains some of its blue, bruised, pulling away. The soft-focus smear of light-pollution around the edges.

The wall-muted neighbor sounds of voices. She finds

the closest tree, its protective bulk. Listens.

Scraps of sound coalesce, a woman's voice: "Idiot." A flinty scrape. "You can't do that here."

A man's voice: "I'm outside."

"Doesn't matter. Where're you gonna toss the butt? In your pocket?"

Vee steps carefully, peers around the tree, sees a lacework of light, the negative space between branches. She inches forward.

"What happened to the midyear resolution, anyway?"

"Roll-your-owns don't count."

"I wish I had a map of your brain's logic. I imagine it'd look like the New York City Subway map."

Through the mistletoe-sharp leaves, she sees Floyd and wife. Mostly outlines, recognizable by Q-ball dome and bouffant-flair, punctuated by the pulsing glow of the former's cigarette-cherry

Floyd says: "The more you pressure me to quit, the more stress I have and the more I need a cigarette to quell my stress."

"I want to leave. I don't care about the protests, I'm not going to be stuck here."

"Riots, babe. Not protests. Agitations."

"I want to leave."

Floyd takes a drag, lets it out. Smoke illuminates needles of light above them like a Las Vegas laser show. The man looks up, as if to bask in the brief glory of his exhale, and for a moment, through the serpentine smoke, his eyes seem to land on hers, then move away. She tucks herself behind the tree again, hears her disturbance of the brush. She bites her lip, feels where it's swelled from before, like a cooked pea beneath soft pulpy skin.

"Go for it." Floyd's voice.

Vee can't see any way by these assholes. To the right, a sharp incline of shadow and snarls of leaves. To the left, a too-dark mess of hazard. Floyd and wife are blocking the only clear path to the tree-house that she can figure.

She bends down, worms her fingers into the dirt. Finds fingernail-clips of ambiguous material. Her hand wraps around a testicle of stone. She pulls it up. She bends, torso-torqued, around the tree. Hurls the stone up and over and past the bickering couple.

Makes a tiny squirrel-rustle on the other side of them. They look.

Floyd's wife calls into the bushes: "Charlie?"

She huffs off toward the sound, pink velour bottom fading into darkness. Floyd follows.

Vee waits until their calls for Charlie—which sound like they're calling for a lost puppy—grow distant, and then she emerges from behind the tree and continues toward the tree-house.

Surely off the path, sounds like she's walking on candy wrappers. Her knees tangle in some sort of thorny thing. Reaches down, finds a bristly branch, the pop-squish of a berry.

Suddenly remembers it's the twenty-first century, pulls out her cell phone, a relic of the twentieth: all flip action and no smart function. Still, the dull glow of its display grants a two-foot access into the dark. About as helpful as opening your eyes in a muddy lake. Good, though, makes her less noticeable as she makes her stumbling way to the tree-house.

She looks at her hands—all that berry juice in the dark-room light of her cell phone, looks like she's been finger-banging a squid.

Finds a branch of something deciduous, fleshy hand-size leaves, vascular and goose-pimpled. Pulls a few off. Wipes her hands clean. Continues walking, clutching the leaves, tearing at them in her palm, thumb digging in. The pulp cold beneath her thumbnail.

Can't see, but really it's not totally dark yet. Just that florae this dense make the crepuscular straight pitch.

She's beginning to gain an odd confidence walking semi-blindly out here. She feels her gait gain a lady-lumberjack strut. As if this whole time all she needed to not be afraid was to not see whatever's in front of her.

Making good foot time, she'll be at the tree-house soon enough. She'll give Charlie his gift, watch him open it, watch him love it, and he'll give her one of those kid-hugs that's somehow dutifully rote and genuinely affectionate at the same impossible time.

She steps past a plant that has a silhouette like Sideshow Bob and sees a lighter, a cigarette's glowing cherry, a man holding both.

She stumbles to a stop.

It's Floyd. Five feet before her. Hands cupped to light a cigarette as if by prayer, smoke sent heavenward.

He turns, and another light emerges. A flashlight tucked between arm and chest, previously hidden by his bulk. It shines a spotlight on his sneakers, shit-scuffed. He puts the lighter in his pocket, grabs the flashlight from his armpit and shines it in Vee's face, cop-like.

Vee feels her stomach go rippley, worries—her perennial fear in moments whiplashed by stress—that she's going to suddenly have the sphincter control of a pigeon, lose it in a hot burst all down her pant-legs.

"There you are," Floyd says.

"Found me."

"Finders keepers."

She adjusts her jacket, stuffs her phone in her pocket. "You talk like a serial killer movie."

"You really know how to stir a ruckus."

"I bring the noise, I suppose."

"So what's your deal here? You trying to sneak out? 'Cause I'd advise it."

She wants one of his cigarettes, wants the authority that comes with brandishing the little flaming white dick of a Marlboro Light. She pictures the pea-size lesion it would leave on his face when she flicks it at him.

"I'm not leaving yet," she says.

Floyd shines his light away and the residual effect on her retina pulses like a purple sun. She has only the use of her peripheral vision now, and Floyd seems to be investigating a nearby patch of something.

"What is this, rice?" he says. "Jesus. They'll try to grow anything here. We had to eat rice every day in the Nav. Used to scatter the uncooked rice onto the deck for the birds to eat. Kept hoping they'd explode with burst bellies when the rice expanded. Kept hoping for a Fourth of July of bird-gut fireworks."

Still slightly blinded, she hears him pissing with impressive force, surely onto the rice paddy.

"Why are you telling me this?"

"Christ, you're testy. I'm just making conversation."

She pushes the heels of her hands into her closed eyes and that purple star in her vision swells, like the sun finally burning itself out, a slowly dilating globe of fire. That old warning, when the sun burns out the Earth will have eight minutes before the awesome destruction breaches our atmosphere. One minute, two minute, three—the comfort of apocalypse—four minute, five minute, six—no need to despair—seven minute—when it's coming for everyone—eight.

She opens her eyes. Floyd is done pissing, now facing her, but has neglected to zip up his jeans, one side flapped open like a lapel.

"I'm just trying to get to the tree-house," she says.

"I ain't seen no tree-house around here."

"It's small."

"How small?"

"About four feet by four feet."

He laughs a stage laugh.

"It's in the cottonwood, over in the corner of the property."

"Fuck's a cottonwood?"

She points dickward. "Barn door's open."

"So," Floyd says and drags the cigarette, "you're trying to get to a tiny tree-house," shows words with smoke.

"X.Y.Z."

"Why don't you just scram? Pam's rousing the wolves for you. What's in the tree-house so important?"

She wonders if that wolf reference just might be literal. Can't be sure in a home that grows untold varietals of jicama.

"So—you just want to get to this tree-house?"

"Then I'll leave."

"Shit, I'll take you to the tree-house."

"You just said you don't know where it is."

"So where is it?"

"Over at the edge of all those fruit trees."

"Follow me." He turns, three-quarters.

"You can't walk with your dick flap open like that."

"Ventilation." He reaches into his pants, makes adjustments. "You don't know what it's like to have balls. They go around all day, constricted, heavy—just need a release valve every now and then." He pulls his hand out, sniffs fingertips.

"My boyfriend—he wears briefs. Says they offer support without constricting. Says constriction is a result of loose fabric, not tight."

"That right."

"That's what my boyfriend says."

"You seem pretty determined to let me know you have a boyfriend."

"Just stating fact. I mean, husband. We got married."

"Uh-huh." He smiles, or at least raises his eyebrows in a way that seems like he's smiling without actually moving his mouth. "Follow me." He walks off, backpack retreating into darkness.

She doesn't move. "My boyfriend, he's gonna pick me up. In his car."

The backpack stops. "Your boyfriend ain't gonna take you to the tree-house. This asshole right here is. So follow."

Follow—such an easy sound, a gently pulling undertow of a sound. But one she's heard enough for it to seem— like your own name repeated into a mirror until it's a purely alien and laughably nonsensical word—meaningless. Absurd.

"You coming?" Floyd's voice, now coming from just beyond the border of dark.

She feels only the dark dilating, moving in, her eye

refusing to adjust.

She steps toward the sound of Floyd's voice, where it seems to be coming from, and perhaps he turns but suddenly the spray of flashlight is there, visible. The pattern of its light seen through branches is like someone has taken scissors to a blank sheet of paper, scattered the bits of geometric bright white onto black felt. She follows.

Catches up to him. He's waiting there, thumb looped onto backpack strap with expectant authority. His pants are still unzipped. He continues walking. She follows the Frankenstein-look of all those fucking zippers on his backpack and the sound of his nostril-whistle.

To her right, above the foliage, the distant light from the house—like that Polaris prop in those shitty Christmas plays their dad forced them into to make up for the other eleven months of church truancy—seems to be getting more distant.

"Aren't we going the wrong way?"

"You're lost," he says.

Rocks underfoot, path gone cobblestone. Branches clawing at her, ineffectual ghouls.

Her Sherpa pushes a branch out of the way and it swings back and thwacks the top of her head with evergreen bristle.

"We're going the wrong way." She stops, pulls twigs from her hair.

The flashlight emerges again in the distance, a single small beam that soon focuses back on her.

"Lemme guess," she says. "You're that guy who always has his high-beams on all the fuckin' time, right?"

She crouches down, in part to eschew the flashlight's sniper-sight, in part to ease the dull ache stretching across her back. Rests her elbows on her knees, her pant-waist cutting into her belly. All relief must be paid for with new pain, the awful economy of the body.

Floyd's light shakes, steadies, shakes. Behind it, the disturbances of dead leaves.

"Shit, dude. Point that thing elsewhere."

The light keeps coming closer. Impossible, though, to tell distance, as that knife-point of light is the only thing her eyes register.

"Dude?"

Between her feet, her hands find the dull prow of a rock, half buried in dirt.

"Why you being all creepy silent all suddenly?"

She pushes her fingers into the earthworm space between soil and stone. Glad for once that Vlad has the bonkers habit of chewing her nails nearly to the quick. The rock is pocked like a moonscape. Grips it, hefts it up.

The light growing, nearing.

She realizes she's face-level for his open fly. Stands up, brings the rock with her. Holding it out before her like a gift.

The light nearing, the breathing behind it now audible.

"Dude—"

The glare in her face is concussive. Eyes closed, even eyelids are just thin meshes of vein. She hefts the rock above her head.

"Dude—"

Can't tell if that's his breath or hers.

The rock is heavy enough to numb the heel of her palms.

Floyd's voice: "The fuck're you—"

Floyd's hand: on her wrist, tight.

She brings the rock down. It finds resistance on, presumably, Floyd's head. Both rock and body drop. A shout like a popped bagpipe.

Flashlight falls away, helicopter blade of light.

She hears him grasping around on the ground. Breathing in moans.

She leans down, reaches for him, grabs an elbow, a forearm. He's holding his head, face. She puts her hands on his chest, hoping to communicate good will, ministration.

"Are you okay? Are you okay?" She incants these words, and hearing them she wants to bash her own head with a rock, but it's all she can do. "Are you okay, areuooookay, arookay."

Her hands touch stubbly face, pull back. She feels the warm viscous something now between her fingers. Hears the backpack ruffle under his weight as he rolls in pain.

The backpack, diapers. Diapers to staunch the blood.

Kneels down, reaches for him. Finds him on his side. Tries to unzip the backpack, but his shoulder, arms, they're in the way. She grabs his wrist, extends his arm and pulls off one strap. Rolls him—his body concussed into compliancy—onto his side and unloops the other strap. Pulls the backpack away from him, unzips, reaches around inside. Impossible to tell what anything is—all toddler paraphernalia is fluid-proofed and so produces the same soft crinkle as diapers.

The flashlight—it's over there, that splotch of visible dirt over there. She walks over, grabs it. Sudden recourse to, control of, simple light—feels epiphanal.

Shines it into the backpack, finds a few diapers there on top, all festooned with pastel animals. Pulls one out.

Walks back over to Floyd: still rolling around in dazed

pain, hands over his head, his face. She sets down the backpack, has the flashlight in one hand, the diaper in the other. With free fingers peels back the diaper tape, unfolds the thing.

Standing over Floyd now, holding him in the light. He rolls onto his back—she holds the diaper out—he uncovers his face—

The mess she made of it, a smear of gore. The horror of his nose, now a displacement of bone at the bridge. A peeled-back gash between his eyes, up into his forehead. One eye shut, the other open and all red like a white rabbit's. His mouth open, lets out a weak moan that inflates a blood bubble at his lips, pops like gum.

She needs to retch, scream, do anything expulsive, purge this sight, this event.

Shaking, she holds the open diaper closer to Floyd's open head. On contact, he grabs her wrist. She jumps back, pulls away, twists herself free, a reaction so snap she can't stop it. She grabs the backpack and runs, finding her way with the flashlight.

At a distance, it feels oddly good, exhilarating in fact to have given her body and actions over to pure instinct—go, id, go!—something primal, existentially vital.

She slows down, realizes she's still clutching the diaper.

Other thoughts. Find others. She needs them. Pure revulsion has played its part, but rationality needs to wrest control again if she's ever going to clear that sight from her brain. Other thoughts.

The backpack, the flashlight. Resources. The light is helpful, sure, but the diaper bag?

What were those tales of survival she read in

childhood? All those stories of industrious kids surviving deserted islands and remote wilderness with nothing but the barest of resources. Like *Hatchet* and *The Black Stallion*. But the characters in those books had it easy. Sure, give her an axe or a fucking stallion and she could do anything, but a diaper bag? Still, those books had a point, and not just to train kids to be MacGyvers, but that survival was a matter of making the most out of precious little. But still, a fucking diaper bag? *Home Alone* might be a better reference point—everyday objects repurposed for warfare. Just takes a little creativity.

She hunkers down under a tree, listens. Can't hear any human sound. Unsure how far from the house she's wandered. She can't see the light on the house. Doesn't make sense. It feels like the yard, confusing and large but still circumscribed, ultimately finite—Pam and Geoff having proved their dominion over nature, folded it like laundry—is now unfurling itself, looping itself, trapping her in its gerbil-wheel of spacetime.

Maybe from her new bounty of resources she can fashion a compass that will restore simple cardinal directions to this mess of space, order and sense, guide her to the tree-house. Though she doesn't know which cardinal direction she'd be looking for.

She roots through the backpack, takes stock.

Diapers, natch. A red sunhat. Tube of sunscreen. A mat, perhaps for changing diapers on. An understudy change of kid-clothes, terry-soft and studded with snaps. A mondo container of hand sanitizer, surely for post-changing ablution. A half-filled squirt gun. A few plastic baggies of Cheerios. A bright blue harness, with buckles and an elastic-laced leash—some sort of bondage device perhaps, mommy and daddy's toy mixed in with the rugrat's? But she sees the embroidered brand: Mommy's Little Helper. This is what's wrong with these assholes—to them Mommy's Little Helper is a purely practical and utilitarian leash with which to keep your kid in heel, rather than the Valium of the Stones song. These people, they're stealing all the good drug references, gelding them, appropriating them into their post-counterculture culture. Jesus.

But for all its practicality, what's she going to do with any of this?

She's all for creativity in application, for Rube Goldberg-ian appropriation of mundania, but how the fuck any of this is going to help her in her mission is utterly beyond her. She wishes she had one of those children's book authors or Hollywood screenwriters with her now for some quick counsel.

But of course there's that secret compartment with the moist wipes. If nothing else, she can clean the blood from her hands.

She finds the wipes. They work pretty well getting the blood off. That Lady Macbeth was full of shit—she just needed some antibacterial chloride and she could've rested easy, stopped all her bitching.

Wait—shit. She can figure out which direction the tree-house is in. She remembers that the house is on a hilltop street that seems to head directly for the bay, west. If standing in the middle of the street, facing the bay, the house would be on your left. Which means the house is facing north. Which means to get back to the house she would have to walk due north. However, when facing away from the back of the house and walking into the backyard farm, the tree-house was slightly to the right. Which means:

shit. What does it mean? That, she thinks, the tree-house is generally in a north/north-west direction from her current position, assuming this ridiculous backyard is a somewhat straight rectangle jutting out from the house. She wishes she had another beer. Okay—north/north-west. Just remember Hitchcock. There's still the question though of how to establish just what north/north-west is.

She feels the horn-blare of confidence and capability fanfare in her chest, and she roots through the backpack again. Anything metal and needley. She knows this one. She can magnetize the metal by rubbing it quickly against her shirt, then setting it on a leaf to float in a puddle of water, and it'll point north, but—there's nothing. Not even a paperclip. Assholes probably scared anything metal would pop and deflate their plump little sprog.

Other thoughts, other ideas. The stars. She can navigate by those things. Sailors did it, why can't she. She's smarter than a bunch of old syphilis-crazed sailors. Except they didn't have to sail through the light-polluted Bay Area. Vee can't see any distant glimmering celestial bodies up there. Just a loose splattering like a few dim Christmas lights that don't form any sort of recognizable shapes much less constellations. Screw Orion, she can't even find a simple rhombus. Still, it would make sense that the brightest of this poor showing would still be the North Star. So *that* one, that one over there, the one that looks like it might actually be an airplane, that one that seems to have a slippery spacial relationship with the rest of the sky, that one that is clearly moving, that one that *is* a plane. Fuck. But it's probably going to or from either SFO or Oakland International, both of which are south-west from here. So she can narrow north down to two options. But which one.

Fuck it. Be decisive. She points into the sky, follows the metronome wag of her finger as it alternates options:

Ip dip doo,
doggy did a poo,
went to the cinema at half-past two.
When the film started,
somebody farted,
and that person's you.

There, she has it, a decision. Ip Dip don't lie. Especially when Ip Dip's decision points her away from whence she came, away from Floyd's awful face, that thing like a Halloween mask in the midst of being ripped off. Broken and torn. That low frequency of his moan still bubbling her marrow.

She stands up, grabs the backpack, starts walking toward the *you*.

She heard a girl recently sing an alternative version of "Ip Dip," something cleansed of its shitting and farting, censored into nonsense. This was at the County of Alameda Clerk-Recorder's Office in downtown Oakland where she and Vlad arrived four minutes before the day's cutoff. They'd come here to do the deed, to sign the deed, to be united in blissful etcetera as Mr. and Mrs. Inhaler.

On the BART ride over, they'd sat silently, leaning against each other, watching a small puddle of soda in the center of the train's aisle, the liquid held in a delicate meniscus. It had found an odd moment of equilibrium on the moving train—twitching in its precarious stability—and as soon as the train slowed to a stop the happy little puddle would resume its helter-skelter path about the train floor. For now, it was just sitting, but the suspense was unbearable.

Now standing in the Clerk-Recorder's foyer, waiting for their number to be called like at a deli, Vlad examined the WPA-era marble floor—wondering aloud about the iconography that, yes, did seem less a celebration of labor and more like what Vlad calls today's post-labor era, a coloring book for a hyperactive boy—while Vee watched the others waiting their turns: the elderly couple in matching rhinestone-studded blue jeans, the old woman holding hands with the young ponytailed guy, tank-top exposing shoulders peeling with sunburn, the solo man standing in front of the flatscreen TV that showed the numbers being called, holding his ticket tightly, looking down at it as every new number popped up on the screen, *now serving 89 at window number 3*, and the little girl who'd clearly been put in charge of two younger kids while their parents were off tending to some bit of bureaucracy. She was pointing to one kid, then the other, singing, "Ip dip doo, my cat's got the flu, swimming in the water, like a ship in a saucer, but you're not in it."

Not only was this girl's version of the rhyme illogical, it ended on a person being *not* it, rather than Vee's version, which elected a person decisively it. It seemed cruel, to be singled out for your exclusion, like an awards presenter announcing to the audience not the winner but rather all the nominees who *didn't* win. Vee felt an impulse to go over, correct this girl, insist on the affirmative pleasure of it-ness, but Vlad was gently squeezing her shoulder, saying, "This is us, babe. Our number's up."

She's been walking for who knows. Flashlight trained on the ground immediate before her. Just trying not to fall.

The backpack strap chafing her neck. She flips up the collar of her surplus jacket bro-style to protect her neck from the polyester strap.

She passes through a cluster of spriggy bushes and shines the flashlight around, looking for anything that might resemble a path. Some foot-trampled leaves, anything.

She points the light on a dark puddle, there at the foot of that tree. Too dark and viscous to be water, like an oil spill. She walks closer, light steady on the puddle. It's red, getting redder as the light gets closer. A drop in the middle, ripples.

She looks up, shines the flashlight directly above the puddle. At first, it just looks like a feathery piñata. There's a shiny rind of cardboard dangling down, and above it the animal seems to be strung up by its feet, twiggy things covered in tiny feathers like a pair of spats. Roosevelt's head seems to be missing, just a bloodletting absence.

She steps forward, tentatively reaches out to the scrap of cardboard. One side is white, the other a glossy blue with a silvery diamond pattern. Torn loose of the whole, but still retaining the curve of the conical party hat. The little elastic chin-band ties the cardboard to Roosevelt's leg.

There's some writing on the inside of the hat scrap. She turns it around to see, careful not to touch the executed animal. In an unsteady scrawl, in blue, wax-spotty crayon, it says, *VEEEE*.

Six.

Backpack smacking the backs of her arms. As she runs. Big high-kicking steps. Doesn't want to trip over something. A root, a rock. Flashlight trained not on the ground but ahead, parting the dark like hands on curtains. That the dark is filled with other things—that there're branches, leaves, fucking tree trunks—doesn't mean the substance she's treading through is nature. It's the dark, liquid and all-filling. These other things, they're just jetsam. If only she could pass as jetsam with them.

Her shoulder scrapes a bit of unidentified jetsam, stings. A reminder that she's the foreign object here. Can't integrate herself into the beautiful anonymity of nature, disappear herself.

Keep going.

Can't breathe. Lungs feel scoured as if by steel wool.

Stops. Plants feet firmly. Soles of her feet vibrate. Simple blood circulation suddenly feeling ectoplasmic. She all-over vibrates, skin tingling needley.

Spits on the ground. Hands on knees, leans over. Spits more. Saliva feels blood-warmed. But she shines the light on the expectorant, sees only poolets of simple, frothy clear.

Still. Her lungs are run raw, surely abraded bloody.

She wants to lie down, needs to lie down. Bury her head in the soft soil. Push until worms navigate her sinuses. Push until silt scrapes clean her brain of all action and imagery.

She needs to keep going. Something's out there.

But she *has* been going. She's been running for god-knows and still hasn't reached anything, as if every step she takes only further dilates the space she's trying to cover.

She can rest for just another second. Sets her knee down, a hand. The soil is more rock-spiked than expected. But she rests, allows herself to collapse, no matter what's behind her.

Just for a second. She sits her ass down on the dirt, reclines, backpack serving as crumply seatback. She can just stay here a moment, then she'll get back up but first she'll just stay here a moment, rest.

She clicks off the flashlight, turns off the visible world and all its awful sights. Exists in a hard-soft tactility. If I can't see you, you can't. Those kids, they have it right. They know to resist the tyranny of object permanence, the eve's-apple of the world beyond your lids, beyond control.

It's quiet.

A few pointy rocks make themselves known beneath her. Comfort has unmasked itself as just the lesser of two discomforts, pain versus movement.

The quiet, it's no longer an absence. The quiet is now an increasing presence. The hush becomes a hushing. A vibrating white noise, the kinetic sound of static, the world blowing into your ear.

Her moment of rest is over—she needs to get up again, go. Pull her jellied limbs back into action.

She tries to pull herself up, rediscover fight or flight. But adrenaline is not the wonder drug it's cracked up to be, and the crash is more like death and despair.

"Hi." A voice, somewhere near, young enough to be angelically androgynous, a disembodied chirp. "Aunt Vee." It's Charlie. Somewhere.

She flicks on the flashlight, pans it across the dark like there's been a prison break. Amongst the shrubs, briar and thicket, she scans two red shoes, heartbreakingly small. Shines the light up to Charlie.

Standing there, standing here.

He blocks the light from his face and she says, "Sorry," shines it away from his eyes. She gets to her feet and rushes to him, hugs his tiny body, ribs like his torso's gripped by a giant skeleton hand. Hugs him with enough force for him to gasp for air.

"Charlie—you're here!"

"Hi."

"How'd you get here? You're here!"

"I think I want cake now."

She grips him by the shoulders, squares her face to his. "We need to keep our voices down."

"Why?"

"Because it's not safe. Out here."

"Why?"

"We just need to keep our voices down. Inside voices. Let's play the whispering game."

"You don't have to whisper inside."

"Library voices. Your mom takes you to the library, right?"

He nods. "The story corner on Sunday nights. Ms. Amy has a guitar."

"How did you get here? Where is here? I thought you went to the tree-house."

He shakes his head. "I wanted to hide in the raspberries."

"We're near the raspberries?"

"Can I have cake now?"

"So you never made it to the tree-house?"

He shakes his head.

"Don't you want your present?"

102

A smile takes over his face.

"That's right," she says. "Can you get us to the tree-house?"

A vigorous nod.

"You can!"

He squirms and she realizes she's squeezing his arms hard enough to feel tendon. "Sorry," she says, relaxing her grip. "Let's go to the tree-house. You lead the way."

"Okay."

"But—listen. We have to proceed very carefully. There's—we're still playing hide and seek, okay? And I—we are—the two of us—we're *it*. People are hunting for us and we can't let them find us."

Charlie smiles, whispers, "Okay."

He begins to head out and is almost immediately submerged into darkness. Vee grabs him. "Hold on." She kneels down and opens up the backpack. Pulls out the Mommy's Little Helper.

Holding the flashlight in her mouth like a safecracker, she buckles the harness around Charlie's chest.

"What're you doing?" he asks. "This is for babies. I grew out of this when I was two." But he doesn't resist. "I'm old enough to unbuckle this myself now. Ask Mommy. Ask her about looking for me at the A's game after I unbuckled myself. That's how come I graduated from it."

She considers this. She unbuckles the straps from his sternum, loosens them a bit for slack, then ties them in the tightest double knot her adult strength can muster.

"Can you untie that?"

He tries, tiny kid fingers failing to find purchase in the knot.

"Good," she says, standing. "Let's go."

She gives the leash a light whip, *andiamo*, and he jaunts off.

This is the kind of following that she could get used to. Mush, mush—she's in charge: leading from the back, not being dragged into the unknown by Floyd—

Floyd. Fuck.

She pulls lightly on the leash, just to let Charlie know she's here. In control.

Dashing through the urban farm, on a one-leashed Adderalled birthday boy.

Over rocks, over roots, through bushes and briar.

Though she's shining the flashlight over his head to illuminate his path, Charlie seems to be operating on pure instinct, navigating the darkness with muscle memory, anticipating every curve and tree before the feeble, jaundiced light even shows it.

She pulls back on the leash, hard. Charlie makes a neck-throttled sound. She reels in the leash, dragging him back to her. She grabs him, lifts him to her chest and hides against a tree trunk, clicking off the flashlight.

Charlie's going to say something, squeal, cry maybe, so she covers his mouth, feels his little nose breathe snot onto her hand.

She heard a voice, saw light up ahead. Must assess the threat before making themselves known.

Charlie is squirmier than Owen, heavier. She shushes him as soothingly as she can.

She hears the disturbance near, breath and footfall. Licks of light on the surrounding trees. This isn't the flat, stable light of a flashlight. This is something alive.

Through a trellis of branches, she can see three or four figures. Small figures. One is holding what looks to be a torch.

They've stopped, seem to be pow-wowing.

"If we spread out, we have a better chance," one says. It's a kid, a boy, not one Vee's familiar with. Though the timbre and lilt of all their voices is basically the same register as a flute-squeak.

"Yeah, spread out," another says. The particular castrato-tone of this one sounds familiar: Owen?

"No! We stick together. She's bigger than us. When we find her, we must attack as a whole. One of us alone, she'd squash you. Did you see her?"

Vee's stomach goes zero-gravity. Floats up into her esophagus.

The leader—the one brandishing the torch. It's Waylon.

She pulls Charlie's face to her neck, feels his panicked breath make her skin go minty. Her mouth to the warm bloom of his ear, she breathes *shhhh*.

"But where are we going?" says the third, unidentified child. "Where is she?"

Owen, suddenly the chatterbox, says, "Yeah."

"We need a plan."

"Quiet!" Waylon says. "I have a plan." The light from the torch jerks forward in emphasis. "The plan is to find her. See how afraid of fire she really is."

"But where?"

"She told Celia to kick me in the balls!" Waylon shouts, voice frayed with the threat of tears. "She told Celia—"

"It's okay, Waylon," says Owen. "Breathe."

Waylon paces, emerges from behind a bush, emerges into full view. Vee holds her breath, clutches Charlie tighter.

105

Charlie seems to get the message: she can feel him hold his breath too.

Waylon is standing seven, maybe eight feet from her. But he's facing away and staring down at the ground. They are in the darkness directly to his left, and his torch, what now appears to be a small baseball bat, the fat end wrapped in a flaming tubesock, is in his left hand, surely obscuring any peripheral awareness he might otherwise have of them. In his contemplative moment, he has let the torch lower a bit. The skull-size ball of flame at its end illuminates his face demonically from below, ensuring that his face is nothing but a play of light and dark, restlessly fighting, stretching features and shrinking them back again.

"We've been searching forever," the other kid says, still hidden behind bushes. "We can't find her. What are we *doing*? It's dark and I'm scared."

Owen says, "I'm getting scared too."

Waylon looks up, searches the sky as if he can see through the light pollution to the constellations that hide themselves from Vee, find special augury in their twinkling.

He says, quietly, "Once more into the yard, my friends, once more." Then, turning around to his two friends, raising his voice: "Or close the gate up with our kicked balls!" He walks toward them. "In peace there's nothing so becomes a boy as games of tag and cartoons," raising the torch, "but when the blast of a foot blows on our balls, then imitate the action of a tiger."

The other two boys walk closer to Waylon, emerge into sight, Owen and the other one, rising to the call.

"Flex your biceps," Waylon says, "boil up your blood, hide girlishness with Hulk-like anger." He bows his arms, seems to grow a foot in height. "Then make your eyes go all angry," holding the flame underneath his face to illuminate his own bulging eyes, "as if you can pop them out of your head like a ping-pong ball launcher."

Waylon walks between the two others, who stand like sentries. He lowers his voice: "Now clench your teeth and flare your nostrils, take a deep breath and stand straight like your mom's measuring your height against the closet wall."

Waylon positions himself in front of them, squares his shoulders. "On, on, you awesomest boys—who are descended from gods of war, G.I. Joes who have in this very yard from morn till dinnertime fought as real American heroes."

He hands little Owen the torch. Owen has to hold it with both hands.

"Because if you fail, you'll prove your fathers are not your fathers and so your mothers whores. Set examples for the younger kids, and teach them how to war. And you, good kids, don't forget: this is Raider Nation—so let's prove it, for there is none of you so weak and pathetic that hath not noble luster in your eyes."

Owen is having trouble holding the torch up, so Waylon grabs it back.

"O I see you stand like pit bulls on leashes, straining upon the start." Waylon raises both his voice and the torch: "The game's afoot—follow your spirit, and upon this charge cry, 'Burn the fat bitch!'"

They repeat, "Burn the fat bitch!" and charge into the dark in divergent directions.

She waits.

Hears their feet patter off.

Feels Charlie's breath steady, calm.

After a safe elapse of silence, she whispers to Charlie, "You okay? We're gonna walk now. Okay?"

She loosens her grip on him just enough to let him nod against her chest.

She sets him down, holds his leash. She kneels beside him, whispers, "Super extra quiet. To the tree-house."

Kid seems to get it—the threat, the stakes: an advanced sense of mortality in this one. He walks on, slowly, heightened awareness of the sort of sounds that could give them away. Vee keeps the flashlight off, puts all her trust in her night-blind guide here.

Suddenly a frantic rustle of feet, somewhere near. Charlie stops. She bumps into him, stops too. The sound of feet approaching with Doppler-like compression and speed. Somewhere from their right, or behind.

She turns, bends to scoop up Charlie—when a force, a ball of energy made of knobby limbs, collides with her legs. A thing struggling around between her legs, buckling them, and she falls forward. Puts her arms out to break her fall, palms Charlie right in the head, falls past him.

On the ground. She feels Charlie scramble away. The leash, dangling around her, slithers off. The other one, the kid who tripped her, is still at her ankles, fighting to get up, out of the mess of human collision and aching knees.

She reaches for him, finds a sinewy shoulder. With her other hand, turns on the flashlight, shines it at her captive.

Owen. Eyes bushbaby-wide, pupils quickly shrinking into pinpricks. His mouth opens in a gasp. Kid is about to scream. She drops the flashlight—beam spotlighting away as it falls—and wraps her hand around his mouth. But not before a little peep of panic lets out.

She grips his mouth hard, but he's still screaming, his

108

muted voice made physical with spit and tongue and teeth against her palm.

What happened to passive Owen the Onanist? What wrought this snarling monster?

She rolls onto her knees and tries to keep the kid pinned to her, firm grip on body and mouth as he struggles. From a kneel she manages to stand. The flashlight is at her feet, but she can't risk letting go of the little alarm in her hands to grab it. She steps on the flashlight, turns it on the ground in the direction Charlie ran. The light, though, only spreads out in a fading cone of illuminated dirt. Doesn't show shit.

Kid's still screaming in her hand. She hears footsteps. Sees flames through the branches, approaching. Making the shadows go spastic, elastic.

She needs the flashlight. She hoists Owen's body under her arm, like a sack of kitty litter, holds him there and keeps a grip on his mouth. Freeing her other hand. She leans down—pain in her legs and back, dull but sharply fissured-through, finally making itself known through the anesthetic of adrenaline—kneels, grabs the flashlight.

Just as Waylon appears in the clearing. In one hand, he holds the torch. In the other, he holds the leash. Charlie a few feet in front.

No need to keep Owen silent now, she lets go of his mouth to get a better grip on his body. She points the flashlight at Waylon. The glare in his eyes the only weapon she has.

"There's no escape!" Waylon says.

"Charlie!" she says. "Are you okay?"

He looks uninjured but captive, scared silent. Waylon jerks the leash back and Charlie falls to the ground. Vee screams. Charlie tries to get back up and Waylon keeps him there, foot on his back.

"Let him go!" Vee shouts.

"Sure thing, your ladyship," Waylon says.

The other kid, third member of Waylon's gang, runs into the clearing out of breath.

"It's not the birthday boy I want," Waylon says. "I want the fat bitch who sent Celia to kick me in the balls. Did you get my message?"

"Your what?"

"You saw what we did to Roosevelt?" Waylon looks at the other kid, says, "Xander. Get a branch." Xander scurries around looking for a branch.

"Just let Charlie go and I'll leave, okay?"

"Not that easy. Pain for pain, fatty."

Xander reemerges with an arm-length branch, knotted and laureled. Waylon holds his own torch to the tip of Xander's. The branch lights, but without the vibrancy of the original. Waylon must have dowsed the tip of his in something.

"I told you," Waylon tells Xander, "she's scared of fire. Advance." And they do, they start advancing on her, torches out. Waylon pulls on the leash, dragging Charlie to his feet. He holds his own torch close to Charlie. "You run for it, and the birthday boy gets it."

Something about those flames, the barely controlled violence of a large flame, it sets off intrusive thoughts, flashes of potential injury, burnt and seared flesh. Imagining the sensation of skin going to bubbles and distilled resin-curls of pain. She's read about the pain of burn, how it doesn't stop, how it comes in waves, unrelenting. The torches are still a few feet away but all she sees are the flames in her face, on her body.

"Wait!" she shouts. She holds up her own hostage. "Any closer and Owen gets it!"

Gets what, exactly, she's not sure, but lines like this just offer themselves to you in a hostage standoff.

Waylon laughs, a flesh-rending sound. "You think I care about little Owen there? We're after you, fatty!"

They continue advancing, Charlie visibly panicking with the torch less than a foot from his face.

Vee says, "Well—I don't care about Charlie. We can drop this whole hostage thing! Think about it—we're not interested in each other's hostage so we can all just walk away. Harm to Owen means nothing to you, and harm to Charlie means nothing to me. So we're even—we got nothing!"

The strategy doesn't work. The kids keep coming at her, except Waylon now drops the leash to hold the torch with two hands, like he's up at bat. Charlie disappears.

She can feel the heat from the torches now. It has a gravity to it. The fear of heights, she remembers, is not the fear of falling but the fear of jumping. Maybe the fear of fire is the fear self-immolation. The final catharsis.

Waylon jabs his torch toward her, a warning feint.

Vee jumps back.

Owen twists in her arms, sends a sharp elbow into her left tit.

She drops him.

Waylon and Xander lunge. Fire hisses by her face. Ignites a nerve like a fuse.

She runs. Arms pumping, flashlight in hand, light like a strobe in the dark. She runs.

She trips. Or slips. Either way, on the ground again,

wind knocked out of her. Lungs seizing. The heels of her palms rubbed raw. Gets to her hands and knees, sees in the oblique glare of the flashlight the braided handle of the leash. Leading off into the dark. She grabs it.

Someone approaching from behind. Fast. She turns, on her back, just as Waylon comes running up with the torch. Flame lighting his bared teeth, red-eyed anger. She turns, rolls back, backpack crunching beneath her—Waylon's practically on top of her now—and she kicks him solid in the solar plexus. Sends him flying back, torch falling away.

Waylon gasping for breath. Torch smoldering in a bed of dry leaves.

Flashlight in one hand, leash in the other, she gets to her feet. Walks toward where the leash leads, but it's suddenly pulled tight. Charlie moving away, probably leading her to the tree-house.

She doesn't pull back on the leash. She follows, lets him lead her wherever he goes. She turns off the flashlight, puts it in her back pocket.

Like walking a pent-up dog, she moves forward while leaning back against the leash, a slight counterweight just so she won't tumble forward. The tension results in her taking long, clomping goose-steppy steps.

She begins to enjoy the rhythm. She begins to enjoy the feeling of ceding control to a small boy pulling her safely through an oily darkness, the trust-fall high of blindly letting go to another.

But the steady pull on the leash now goes to staccato tuggings. Charlie's fighting to free himself from Vee's rein. The pull on the leash gets increasingly violent, in erratic directions, with a soundtrack of frustrated grunting, the kid kind of grunting that rips into crying.

She slows. Pulls back on the leash, brings them both to a stop. Reeling the leash in, hand over hand, she moves toward him, calibrating her walking with her leash-reeling.

Closing in on the sound of snot-bubbled kid-sniffles, she holds the leash with one hand, reaches out with the other. Charlie's not trying to run away anymore, and her hand finds his bony scapula.

She kneels down. She considers turning the flashlight on, but has no desire to cast in ghoulish chiaroscuro the bawling face of a boy devastated—of course—by her betrayal, his upper lip surely mustachioed with teary snot. He's probably thankful for the dark. She keeps the flashlight holstered in her pocket.

Kid's crying so hard now it's convulsive, choking. She rubs his back, his buckley spine.

There're things to say, surely. She could explain her botched strategy, the deceit necessary to the genre of hostage negotiation. She could explain that of course she cares about him. She could explain that of course *of course* should never precede *I care*, that care can never be tacit, that a statement trying to make supposed tacitness explicit is bullshit and evasive and indefensible. She could tell him that her hostage-negotiation tactic of negating all concern for him amounted to nothing more than her wresting control of him, of his story, appropriating him for her own selfish purposes. She could say how terribly she just wants Charlie to turn around, see her, release her from the role the world seems to have rigged for her. She could say that she just wants, once, to do this thing that everyone else does so promiscuously: to make a single, small, transitory connection.

She takes off the backpack, sets it down. She unzips

it, feels around inside. Below all the pee-safe garments of toddler-care she finds the plastic baggies of Cheerios.

She touches his shoulder, gently pulls, and he turns around. She finds his hands with her hands and gives him the baggie.

She hears him open the bag. Then the light crunch of him chewing, the sounds pock and pixilate the still air between them, fuzzing the vacuum dark with a pleasant static.

He's eating. She finds the knot of his harness and, with pained fingers wedging into plastic straps pulled tight, she undoes the knot, takes off the harness.

It was Vlad who taught her the tyranny of *of course*—the stating emphatically that what you're saying should not have to be said at all, its subtle ability to quiet.

They were at Quickly's, their agreed-upon favorite tavern within stumbling distance of their new home. Quickly's is a window-shuttered place lit mostly by the glowing screen of the ATM, the Game Boy-looking thing frequented only by the tech-bros who have been showing up in increasing numbers and are incensed by the cash-only policy. These are the guys who ask the bartender why he hasn't heard of this or that *super easy* credit card processing app, and eventually leave via car service. Vlad has a particularly advanced hatred for these types, his understanding of their awfulness developed to the point of being a cogent taxonomy. Most of the offenders have been infiltrating a nearby warehouse space—"like maggots in a trashcan," Vlad said—that was recently flipped into a startup of some sort, which, as far as they could tell from the bits of conversation that now flew like shrapnel in the once-calm Quickly's, specialized in leveraging untapped markets or some such shit. "Building nothing out of something," Vlad said.

Last night, she and Vlad arrived at Quickly's to find their usual booth occupied by bros in clothes casual enough to flaunt the hip and un-uniformed work environment that seemed to be another marker of the new tech overlords, while nice enough to telegraph well-paid employment, responsibility, status high enough on the social hierarchy to make their patronizing of Quickly's just that: patronizing, condescending slumming, reducing the establishment and its longtime clients to mere props of tourism, turning the real into the kitsch.

Vlad waxed vitriolically as much while they stood at the corner of the bar with their whiskies.

"Babe," Vee said, in peacemaker mode, just wanting a relaxing night, "they're entrepreneurs—so are we."

Vlad downed his drink, crunched ice between teeth, looked at her. "They operate legally within unethical laws. We operate illegally outside that same system. Don't apologize for them. Besides, I want my fucking booth."

"We're new to this neighborhood too. It's not like it was our booth to begin with." She was referring to the old black guy who used to sit there all hours reading decades-old issues of *Mad Magazine*, until Vlad convinced him that he would be more comfortable reading at the bar where there was better light. The man agreed, or rather complied— Vlad can be very convincing—but then stopped coming in.

"Besides," Vee said, "those tech guys are probably going to be our customers."

"Not unless we seed our crop with Adderall. Mulch up

pages—what's that book? How to be an asshole and make money?"

"*How To Win Friends and Influence People*," Vee said. (She'd skimmed through a copy her first semester of college, standing in the student bookstore, mostly interested in the promise of the winning friends part, but all she could glean from it was to repeat people's names back at them. The only time she'd tried this, flirting with the guy at the Hot Dog on a Stick counter, he'd finally said, "Listen, this isn't my real nametag. I mean, do I really look like a *Steven*?")

"Yeah," Vlad said, "like if we mulch up pages of those type of books and put that in the soil—then maybe. Whatever, you see what I'm saying."

One of the tech-bros in question got up from their booth and walked up to the bar. When he couldn't get the bartender's attention, he turned to Vlad and Vee and asked, "You know where the restrooms are?"

Vee was about to point to the corner door when Vlad said, "Yeah, they just have a compost heap out in the alley. You have to squat over it. You know, back to the earth. Sustainable."

The guy chuckled, unsure.

"Seriously," Vlad continued, "we're not advanced enough here for plumbing. Guys like you might be used to doing things like shitting in porcelain toilets and orchestrating the economic crash, but we're simple folks here."

The guy's smile faded, and he retreated to find the toilet on his own.

Vee said, "Babe—"

"Did you hear that?"

"What?"

"The fucking—the fucking guy—he called you fat. As he walked away." Vlad put his hands on the bar, leaned in, bracing his anger against the bar's solidity.

"I don't think he did, babe."

"I can't fucking believe it. I can't—" Knuckles white gripping the bar. "How fucking dare he."

"I don't think he said anything. I didn't hear him. Babe, are you listening to—"

"Of course I'm listening!"

That phrase, *of course*, doing its thing, shutting up. It didn't matter. This was his story now, to do with what he pleased, to satisfy whatever he needed to satisfy. Vee's version, Vee herself at this point, and the words real or imagined that gave her body a shape in the world far more than her actual flesh seemed to, had been, in that moment, commandeered for his purposes.

He picked up his glass, slammed its solid base back down, then walked off toward the bathroom.

She feels a tiny hand at her lips. The dry puffed toroid of a Cheerio between fingers. Charlie is feeding her. She eats.

They eat. Together in the dark.

But the dark is fading, or lightening. Charlie's face— its basic shape and outline of features—is emerging. Not, however, in the deep blues that would suggest her eyes are merely adjusting to the night. His face is emerging in colors at the other end of the spectrum. Rich reds, highlights of orange.

He's now clear enough that she can see him wipe away some tear-snot with the back of his wrist.

It feels like the sun is suddenly coming up, with frightening speed.

117

Charlie smiles, then seems to register something worrisome in his aunt's face. "What?"

She hears it: a distant crackle. She stands up.

Sees the trees backlit with a pulsing red. Smells smoke.

She grabs Charlie's hand. Lifts him up onto her shoulders.

She asks, "Can you see anything?"

He holds onto her head, tight.

"It's on fire."

Seven.

Boy on her shoulders, back of his sneakers bumping against her chest as she walks. His hands are clamped onto her skull, thumbs on temples.

She says, "Charlie, babe, I know you're nervous but you're giving me a concussion. Here, hold my hands." She reaches up and takes his hands. He squeezes them hard.

Galvanized by the sight of the fire, they need to move, need to exorcise with exercise, but there's no clear destination. She's just walking, rapidly but timidly. The fire—the sight of it, back there, beyond the bushes, the flames themselves having only consumed a small tree or two but the reach of its dire and fitful light immense, making the once-stable earth seem elastic, mutable—has disoriented her sense of space, kinked the clear map she had in her head, that simple line connecting them and the tree-house.

"Charlie," she says, "Charlie, where do we go? Where do we go, Charlie?"

"Tree-house."

"Your present."

"Tree-house."

"Is it safe? Where is it? Is it away from the fire or towards it? Lead me, Charlie."

"Forward. It's away from fire. It's safe."

"Okay," she says, walking. "I'm gonna get you there, Charlie. I promise. And I'm gonna get you your present. We're gonna be safe, and you're gonna like your present. I promise. Do you know what an amphicoelias is?"

She's on it: Operation Distract The Kid From

119

Danger—which has pleasant crossover with Operation Distract Self From Fear of Massive Fucking Fire.

"No."

"An amphicoelias was the biggest damn dinosaur that ever existed." She's navigating the unpredictable landscape with high, generous steps, as if walking through mud, anticipating rocks and tripwire roots. "He looks a lot like a brontosaurus," she says. "You know the brontosaurus?"

"Yeah. I like those."

"Charlie, an amphicoelias is so much better than a brontosaurus. He looks a lot like one, but he's so much bigger. Huge. So big your brain can't even imagine it. You know a football field? Almost as big as that. To even think about how big an amphicoelias really is, it makes you feel so small, so insignificant, like staring into the Milky Way. They're beautiful, the curve of their body, big enough to feel the curve of the earth, to grip the earth head to tail and palm it like a basketball."

"Adults," Charlie whispers, squeezing her hands, "adults."

She stops, listens.

Sure enough, she hears them, the adults. They're near. Talking in their conspiratorial tones, their treble-tinged passivity and bass-line aggressions.

"They're here," someone says. "Think about it. They must have breached the perimeter."

"But with such stealth?" another says. "These rioters are not known for their subtlety."

"Think about it! Their M.O.!"

"They're emo? No, my nephew is emo and he sits in his room all day too sad to move. These, these *people*, they're anarchists."

120

"Not emo, asshole—*em, oh*, modus operandi. This destruction? It has all the marks of *them*!"

"She's right. All this smacks of them—Floyd, the fire. Look—CitiWatch geotags them in this neighborhood! Look—updated four minutes ago!"

Floyd, *fuck*—the horror of his face, the mess she made of him. This sight of him confirmation of everything she's feared—her monstrousness.

The adults, this Greek chorus of guilt, they seem to be just beyond those trees up there. To her right is a hovel of flora and shrubbery. She steps delicately, almost silently, into its cover.

"But," someone says, "did Floyd say who did it? He might have a description. Ariel does art therapy—maybe she can whip up a, you know, like an artist's rendering? She does amazing charcoal portraits."

"I don't think we'll have any trouble spotting the culprits. I mean, I'm not racist—you know me—but come on."

"How much time do you think we have here? The fucking yard's on fire! And you want to settle in for a cozy mystery?"

"She's right—we need to call someone."

"Hasn't someone already called someone? I mean, I always assume. Surely someone has called someone."

"Can't you do that on CitiWatch? Isn't there a *911* button to click or something?"

"Depends which version you have."

"Also depends on which device you have."

"People, the fucking yard is on fucking fire."

"Language, Tom, language. C'mon, the kids."

"Pam collected the kids."

"Did they find Charlie?"

"I have CitiWatch 3.0—which generation is that?"

"There should—lemme see—there should be a thing here, in the home-screen, here it is. If you click that, it's a direct line to the cops. That's why the button's a red phone, like in the old *Batman*? Remember that?"

"Totally."

"Guys, the—the fire! There's a fire! It's growing!"

Whoever that is is right. Vee can't see it, but she can see the reach of its light, and it's clearly growing. The little hovel she and Charlie are holing themselves up in was a moment ago pitch black, but she can now see the dark sketch of its contours, the crosshatchings of branches. She can feel the heat like a flush of fever.

"But what about Floyd? Has he said anything? I mean—?"

"He's inside. Unconscious, but Quentin is treating his wounds—guy used to be an EMT or something."

"But if he's concussed and he falls asleep—aren't you not supposed to let people with concussions fall asleep?"

"The fuck are you asking me for?"

"Language, Phil, language. Please, the kids."

"Guys, the fire!"

"I think I got it! The red phone button. I clicked it. Does that mean the cops're coming?"

"Guys, the fire."

Charlie is leaning down, hugging her neck, breathing into her ear. She tries to loosen his grip on her neck.

She thinks it's her heart again—an arrhythmia or something. The final beat, the major cardiac episode that the world has told her is inevitable. But no. It's another helicopter, descending upon them. Spotlights placed nipple-like on its hull blind them from seeing the actual thing, but it's there, a presence doing a palpable violence to the atmosphere, the blades sounding like they're shredding spacetime, each beat equal parts noise and the vacuum-silence the preceding laceration exposes.

It's dizzy-making and Charlie is wrapped terrified around her skull like a helmet.

The spotlights from above scan the pathway just outside their hovel. She can see a few of the adults scatter, cockroach-like.

She thinks Charlie might be screaming in her ear, but it could be the helicopter, as there is simply no frequency it is not vibrating. It's right above them. She needs to get them out of here. The fire seems soft and inviting compared to this thing above them, this flying tank. She figures enough adults are fleeing in the god's-eye glare of the copter's searchlights and being one of them is better than being trapped here and the adults themselves are surely too scared now between fire and rioters and potential police action to care about her and her transgressions, so she grips Charlie's thighs tight against her shoulders and bolts out of their hidey hovel and into the light that's so bright and loud it feels like an eye-exam on a firing range, and Charlie's fingers gouge into her head, but she runs, at first back toward the fire because it's away from the copter, filing in with the lemming scramble of a few adults, but Charlie, apparently lucid enough in his fear, or maybe his fear has laser-honed his lucidity, yanks her head to the left like it's a steering wheel, forcing her to turn down a heretofore unseen route.

Safely in the cover of an untrodden path, something

pops in her knee, a little chime of pain, and she slows. Her bra's underwire feels like it's strangling her boobs, and she's pretty sure all this running has caused her pants to chafe her waist bloody, and she wants to vomit, but she keeps moving—she has Charlie, a mission—the pinging hurt in her knee not crippling but like a quiet radar blip of approaching doom.

She keeps going, Charlie reaching out to part the branches from their faces. The helicopter lights behind them or beside them or somewhere are so bright that the branch-barbed path is a high-contrast black and white, and the lines sear too readily onto her retina, clinging in tracers as she closes her eyes or looks away, a beautiful blindness.

They burst into a clearing. See the fire, the size of a house, just over there, in the background, twenty feet, thirty, its heat like a sunburn on her face. In the foreground, a man, standing impotently. He turns, scared. It's Ryan, moustache so greased it looks flammable. His eyebrows twitch eager at her and he moves at her, fast like a lunge.

She twists back into the briar and fights through, fuck the path. Branches clawing at her, at Charlie, whose screaming she can definitely distinguish from the noise of the copter now. She stops. The branches like skeleton hands on their bodies.

"The fire," Charlie says. "It's getting bigger."

She unloops one shoulderstrap of the backpack, unzips and finds the squirt gun. She shakes it, hears sloshing. She hands the squirt gun, cocked and loaded, up to Charlie.

She says, "What do you do if you see fire?"

"Squirt."

"Good kid."

She keeps moving, slower now. Taking care to move the

124

branches with hands not velocity. The light ahead, shining between branches in strings of sheer glare—it's unclear if it's from the fire or the copter or god-willing the single beaconing light on Pam and Geoff's house, hard to believe that house is still even here, the yard having seemingly stretched and distorted so far beyond the territory of the bungalow's shadow, the simple geometry destroyed, but the house must be up ahead somewhere. Either the house or the fire. Unless the two have become one.

And above her, on her shoulders, pulling with one hand his way through these same talon-like branches, is Charlie, who, in his other hand, is wielding a squirt-gun, neon green and filled with a few ounces of Berkeley tap—vauntedly clean, from the Sierras they say, but devastatingly ineffectual against anything other than a candle light, and considering there's what promises to be a fucking fire slowly surrounding them, she's done nothing less than ask this poor child with his sponge-like brain to trust in the magical thinking of his own ability to halt this whirlpooling catastrophe. She might as well have given him a rabbit's foot or horseshoe and told him it had the verifiable, scientifically proven ability to reverse the descent of entropy. She might as well have given him the golden calf of a crucifix and told him about salvation and redemption. No, Charlie, that thing, that piece of toxic slave-made plastic, it is no more effective than we are in this world.

And yet she longs for it, longs to hold that stupid toy herself, longs for the forgotten hope of agency and talismanic action, longs for the pure magical power of it, and so she says, "Charlie, you see fire, you just point and squirt, babe. You just fuckin' shoot at it."

"Fuckin' shoot," he says.

She steps on the wet slosh of what feels like rotten fruit and emerges into a clearing, sees the orange tree, the tire swing, the chicken coop. No chickens, though, surely hiding by now.

Beside the coop is an artichoke plant's hysterical foliage, and just beyond that a blurry blonde head emerges. Blurred, it seems, by smoke. There's enough of it now, moving in tangles, making the wind a visible thing. Charlie coughs, dry and weak; he sounds unable to breathe deeply enough to give the cough any expectory propulsion.

The blonde behind the artichokes, it's Pam and she's looking right at them. Vee can see her older sister's irises contract like F-stops around her pupils, sharpening them to points, or at least she thinks she can see that, zooming in across the distance—or maybe Vee's just remembering some kidhood memory of her sister's eyes, the green-gold webwork of her irises as they squeezed the dark out of her pupils: a distinct memory, though she can't remember the last time she was close enough to see her sister's eye's in such detail.

Pam trounces over her artichoke plants and is shouting something at them and holding out her arms, her hands, elbows and knees moving as if trying to throw off shackles as she walk-runs, now just runs, right for them.

Charlie shouts: "Mommy!" He makes like he's running toward her and repeatedly heels Vee's chest. He struggles on Vee's shoulders, clamoring to get down, pushing off her body to leverage his own body out toward his mom, and in his endeavor to do so, and in Vee's endeavor to restrain him, she somehow sustains flailing knees and feet to the shoulder and esophagus, but in a moment—the same

126

moment that Pam arrives—he's successfully off Vee's shoulders, on the ground, though she's managed to keep a hold of his hand.

"Give!" Pam grabs Charlie's arm, pulls, yanks. She screams, "Gimme," pulling taut even the wavelength of that last long *eee*.

Vee pulls back. She has a grip on the left wrist and her sister has a grip on the right wrist. Vee pulls, Pam pulls. Charlie's arms are strung between the sisters, the rest of his body left to dangle like laundry on a line.

In the tug-of-war, Vee is trying to say something, but all language cedes to the grunt-struggles of simple breathing.

Charlie, though, he still has language, and he shouts to let him go, let him go, this thing between them suddenly freeing itself, twisting out of their grips, Vee managing to get only a fingerling purchase of his shirt elastic, which doesn't hold him back at all, only snaps from her pinch when pulled by his fleeing body as if to add to his propulsion, as if she's just shot him from a slingshot. And there he goes, running away, off across the clearing, toward the chicken coop.

Pam shouts: "Look what you've done!"

Pam shoves Vee. Vee stumbles back.

"Why are you doing this? Why are you—?"

Pam's question-marks have always been more scythe-shaped than curious, and she slices a few more through the air. "Why?"

Vee stands. She's wants to speak, do something, but is aware only of her body standing right here, the atmosphere she's displacing.

"I invited you. To my home. I invited you."

Vee says: "I don't need an invitation. I'm here, Pam."

But Pam is already looking away—off toward the coop, scanning for Charlie, who's fled from sight.

Pam runs across the clearing, head low and panning for the child.

As she runs, her shadow shifts, disappears entirely, and the sound of the helicopter engine shreds the air. The thing is hovering right above them now, and Pam stops, looks up, hands against the light, looking like she's about to be abducted, her hair tossed around like the air is trying to pull it off.

A rope drops, its considerable slack hitting the ground and sending up a poof of dirt just a few feet from Pam. The rope jerks and from the light of the helicopter a figure rappels down on it, feet planting firmly in the dirt. He looks like a G.I. Joe. Heavy boots below what looks to be black leg-guards, like what baseball catchers wear, Teflon-looking chest-plate above that, and arms equally protected beneath scalloped shells of armor. His waist is a collection of weaponry, and the butt of a rifle pokes out from behind him. His helmet extends down in a tinted visor, which is molded into the snout of a gas mask.

Here is a man completely obscured in arms and armor, a Robocop, a man whose status as such is left to guesswork, something best left to a Turing test.

He lets go of the rope and pulls an automatic rifle up from his side. It's one of those ones with the boomerang-shaped reserve of ammo sloping out the bottom.

He's facing forty-five degrees away from Vee and she has no idea if he—or it?—can see her.

Vee spots Charlie watching from behind the coop. Maybe Pam sees him too because she gasps, a belated gasp that looks to suck in much-needed air, and in her scramble the stormtrooper turns to her, rifle pointed down and away, but ready.

The stormtrooper just watching Pam in her paralysis of fear, the two look to be in a stand-off.

A few adults—including sweat-glazed Geoff—run up to the scene, and the stormtrooper makes his first sign of sentience: startled, he lifts his gun with one arm and shoves Pam out of the way with the other, to hold the new arrivals at the business end of his issue. Pam hits the ground, and Geoff and the others raise their hands—*really* raise their hands, not the shoulder-level game of pattycake people play when at gunpoint in the movies: Geoff in particular is reaching so high it looks like his body is being stretched taller by the wrists, and on the ground his wife raises her dirt-caked face.

Charlie runs out from behind the coop, and now there he is, out there, in the alien spotlight of the helicopter, standing before the stormtrooper, an ant challenging the Empire State Building, and he's pointing his gun, his sloshy squirt gun, up at the stormtrooper, yelling something, demanding something—righteously invoking a child's pure sense of justice—and in the moment the stormtrooper turns the ninety degrees from his previous target to this new pint-size one, Pam grabs the man's armadillo-armored ankle and pulls, and so when the stormtrooper opens fire on this boy who's threatening him with a gun, a gun with its toy-spit of water, the stormtrooper wobbles and his gun, his real gun, tilts and the three shots that puncture the air miss the child, presumably go just above his head.

Screams follow the gunshots like the rippling wakes of the bullets themselves, and Charlie runs for it, runs back to the chicken coop, dashes up the ramp and right inside.

The stormtrooper charges toward the coop—Pam still gripping his ankle, dragged a few feet till he shakes her loose.

The stormtrooper positions himself just outside of the coop, three-quarters angled at his target, gun up.

Vee can hear the bass-rumble of him shouting something, the cadence of a command, but the helicopter engine absorbs the treble and specifics of his words.

Geoff runs up to Pam, comforts her on the ground. The two of them coiled around each other and pleading with the stormtrooper, Pam pawing at the dirt, Geoff, herself. Her face red, her neck arterial.

Vee turns around, folds herself to the ground behind a tree. The backpack snags on a branch, rides up, and a strap scrapes her ear. She pulls the backpack off, clutches it to her chest. Squeezes it for all it's worth, feels the odd geometry of its contents.

She sets it down, unzips, looks inside. She grabs the hand sanitizer. She grabs the other Ziplock of Cheerios.

What sounds like a bullhorn from above announces, "Exit the construction with your hands in the air."

She empties the Cheerios out of the bag. She twists off the cap to the hand sanitizer. She squeezes half of it out into the Ziplock until the baggie is filled with the clear bubble-pocked gel. Holding it feels like how she imagines a silicone implant would feel.

"Exit the construction with your hands in the air or our ground agent will open fire."

She rips a strip of fabric off the lining of her shirt, about six inches. She closes the Ziplock around the strip of fabric, half of it flapping out. She rubs that end with some residual hand sanitizer. She fishes in her pocket for her lighter.

A few shots are fired. She can hear the steel-drum sound of the rounds hitting the chicken coop.

She lights the wick of the makeshift Molotov cocktail, stands up and launches the thing at the stormtrooper. It bursts against his back and the splatter ignites like napalm.

The flame isn't the garish orange of the nearing fire—rather, it's a dim aura of blue over his back. He lowers his gun, slowly, curiously. Looks over his shoulder to see the liquid ripple creeping up his shoulder. On him, fire seems to have a clearer substance. There's a rivulet of fire down his right arm. He takes his right hand off the gun and holds his arm up to his helmet-obscured face, turns it around, watches the shimmering blue flame as if hypnotized.

Behind him, in a freshly bullet-holed chicken coop, Charlie peeks his head out, watches. Pam and Geoff also look lobotomized in awe.

The stormtrooper turns and sees Vee—not holding anything incriminating but surely looking culpable somehow. She runs for it.

Back through the tangle and snarl of branches, sharp and clawing at her, excoriating and stabby, she moves as fast as she can.

She emerges into a glade walled on one side by the fire. She can feel it, this slithery stuff of fire, attempting to bubble her flesh, dry-boil her body. Her hairs singeing up into curlicues of toxic smoke. For a moment, she gives herself into it, fear giving way to comfort in the inevitability of immolation.

But then the stormtrooper appears. Enters stage-right. She backs up, backs into the briar. The stormtrooper walks calmly across her path, his darkened visor surely limiting his peripheral vision, in which Vee hides amongst the flora that quivers in the heat-rippled air.

The man is still casually aflame like the Human Torch, but it burns tight to his body, never growing into obscene oranges or reds. He moves in a gloss of blue, moves androidally unafraid of the fire, is partially made of it now. He's scanning for her. Firearm at the ready.

She has to keep still, even while the air itself is investigating every nerve ending with a blowtorch.

As the stormtrooper moves slowly across the scene, she tries to go Zen with the pain, fails. It's real and it's on her like meth-addled fire ants. She needs to move, needs to exorcise the pain by either running headfirst into the fire that is filling her lungs with its Chernobyl-breath, or run back into the cluster of safely not-on-fire branches.

Just as she thinks she's going to snap, to shatter into shards, the stormtrooper has passed, is gone, off into the darkness again, continuing his search.

Again, she runs. Runs away from the fire, away from the stormtrooper, finds a path not barbed by nature, just the pillowing, cooling, salving air.

She can run it off, run off the pain, run off what she's seen, done.

She can.

She can run until her velocity peels back this fucking urban farm to find the primordial, and she can out run time and self and circumstance, into something as pure as the needle-point lights of pain that still, despite the running and the air, illuminate her flesh, and she smacks, face-first, right into something solid, something like a tree-trunk but lacking the hard calluses of bark, and she falls back, her face concussed numb, falls onto her back, onto the ground, its whiplashing solidity, knocking the wind out of her, lungs squeezed as if by a fist.

Supine, she's spent.

Seems like an epoch ago but it was just this morning when she woke up to Vlad crying, muffledly. He was beside her in bed. The pillow seemed to be stuck to his face. She'd told him the night before to sleep on his side, but he always sleeps face-down and now the blood from his punched-in nose, punched in by the tech-bro, had dried and glued his face to the pillow and he was screaming that he couldn't see, that he was blind.

"You're not blind, baby. It's just the pillow."

The thing was stuck to him like a permanent airbag and she had to lead him to the bathroom and stand with him in the hot shower until she could peel that soaked pillow, heavy with water, from his face, then wash from his face— *careful, careful!*—the goopy blood now oxidized brown.

"See?" he said. "I'm not like them." He pointed at his own broken face, his mangled nose and swollen-shut eye, showed her a blood-dark smile. "Mark of the oppressed."

"Baby," she said. "I think you're still bleeding. I think we need to get you to a doctor."

She drove him to the nearest Urgent Care and waited in the plastic-fern lobby watching local news, a white bandana held to his nose, slowly tie-dyed red, and when he was finally able to be seen she had to go, had to go to Charlie's party.

"I gotta go do the family thing," she said. "If I take the car, can you get a bus home?"

"I'll get an Uber. Go, have fun."

133

So she left him there, left him to the nurse in the Hello Kitty scrubs, and when he called out that he loved her as she was exiting the sliding glass doors it didn't occur to her until minutes later that she didn't respond to, much less acknowledge, his rote affection—the emptied language that she had before been so eager to fill with her own conviction now best left hollow.

She drove toward her sister's house, through West Oakland and its post-industrial flatlands, until the buildings reached higher, with grander neoclassical ambitions for cityhood, and now she was in downtown and there was traffic. Not just cars but people. People congesting the streets.

They were painting the names of the dead onto the walls of the city buildings, until they ran out of room and they began painting the names of the dead onto all the walls everywhere.

Traffic halted. In front of her, the sandy-haired man in the car sporting a *Free Leonard* bumper sticker began honking, yelling out the window about being late for work. People walking through the traffic as if through aisles in a grocery store, on their way to City Hall. Vee rolled her window down, listened.

Like the discord of a symphony warming up and eventually coalescing into rhythm and melody and harmony, the voices outside began to unify into a chant. Its downbeat was "we," accumulating voices with each refrain, and, windows down, beating her fist against the steering wheel to the crowd's staccato, Vee started chanting along. But that downbeat, that "we," it curdled in her mouth. Or rather, her mouth curdled around it. Outside, the sidewalks overflowing, the names of the dead proliferating with devastating speed on the walls of the city, the chant growing with an overwhelming anger, an anger that she could not—that no one she knows—could lay legitimate claim to. Anger was always a reassuring recourse for her, for the people she gravitated mostly to, if not an anger expressed than at least an anger held tightly to her chest, reassuring her. But, here was a despair wholly inaccessible to her, and to attempt to fit herself into it was to do a violence to that anger, to its rightness and sanctity.

When, after the traffic crept out of the increasingly dense nucleolus of the growing protest and she eventually made it all the way up to Berkeley, she parked outside her sister's house, which, with its low flat gable, resembled a man's face with a ball-cap pulled far down, to hide identity beneath the brim, and she pulled the one-hitter from her pocket, packed it, flicked her little lighter, the satisfying flint-scrape followed by the familiar little fear-twitch when the flame caught, and she sucked the fire into the green-swirled glass pipe. She filled her lungs, waited for her body to calm, waited for the THC to sink in, eventually feeling it come like ink diluting into water, exhaled.

She pulled the gift-wrapped box from the backseat, imagined Charlie's smile when she would give it to him, imagined Pam's smile, imagined Pam wondering what this new thing creeping across her face was, this thing called a smile, this strange force distorting her facial muscles, and Vee laughed to herself, puffing out a trace of smoke that had been stowing away in errant bronchial pockets.

She got out of the car and walked toward the house.

She's on the ground, skull like a maraca from the impact and fall. She looks up at the tree she collided with: it's giant, a redwood or sequoia, something large enough and old enough—because trees kindly conform to the kid-logic of conflating size and age and wisdom—that a cross-section would surely show tree-rings dating back millennia, time-travel a simple slide of the finger, spacetime squashed into a flatland of concentric circles, dimensionality just a conceit of aesthetics—and she sees the supple scales of its bark, sees it flex.

In the penumbra light of the fire, she can see this trunk-like thing stretch up into the dark, curve out of sight. The curve starts to move. Down toward her. Something, a head it seems the size of a city bus, emerges from above to peer down at her. It sniffs.

"Oh," she says. "Hi."

Eight.

She's at the cottonwood tree, the tree-house above. She's finally here and she's out of breath, hands against the trunk, bracing herself and breathing. The helicopter seems farther away now—she can still hear its throbbing propeller but there's now room in her brain for thought, and she can see the bark of the tree by the light of the nearby fire, which is a pleasant blush compared to the halogen blast from the copter.

She can feel the open-oven warmth of the fire but can't tell where exactly it is. It's just around, all around, in the wings, waiting. She squeezes the tree, feels its solidity, scrapes little lines into it with her fingernails. Her hands need a moment to readjust to this kind of hardness, its blunt insistency. The creature, when she touched him, there was the pretense of something hard, but beneath it, life. Its armor was undeniable, cauterized against the world, but she pushed against, tested it, felt the softness of life. In just that moment or maybe it was an hour or an epoch she accustomed herself to the beast's ambivalent flesh, and now here she is holding the base of a cottonwood tree, instinctively searching for that same life.

"Aunt Vee!" Charlie's voice, from above.

"Charlie! You made it!"

His face is peering down over the edge of her stupidly simple tree-house, those three planks screwed together into a splintery square. But there he is, Charlie, his face just visible from the nose up, his little hands holding the edge, like a *Kilroy Was Here* doodle a soldier has left behind on a scrap of devastation.

137

"You said to go to the tree-house."

"I did."

"So I did."

"I love you!"

She climbs. She grabs hold of the extra scraps of wood that she screwed into the trunk as rungs some four years ago, and she climbs. It's not easy. The rungs are not deep enough to get her body weight comfortably on them. She has to get her body flat against the tree and clamp her fingers on the rungs as tightly as possible.

She can still feel the accordion rise-and-fall of the creature's body as it breathed beneath her, residual in her body like the waves beneath a sailor's feet long after docking. The creature's body, when she was atop it, was so massive its breathing was more tectonic than anything, its body a new land.

Her fingers clamping down on the wooden rungs screwed to the trunk, there's a sudden pinched pain between fingernail and finger. She's unsure but it feels like a splinter has insinuated itself into the tender fingerpulp beneath her already gnawed-raw nails. Feels like it's driving itself in there. She wants to let go, stick her finger into her mouth to salve, but she's high enough up the trunk now and she needs both hands. Has to keep going.

The *keep going* was the key, the beauty of that creature, immune to not just splinters with its thick flesh but also to the mere notion of stopping, movement a pure expression of instinct, its depth and reach, movement as vital as orbit.

Her foot slips from one particularly feeble rung and she grabs the tree like a hug and slides down—her cheek scraping against the bark and maybe the extruded heel of a screw—until she manages a saving toe-grip on the next rung below, and she hears Charlie above ask if she's okay and she says yes, yes, and she steadies herself—a moment of stillness, her and the tree—and then reaches up again to keep climbing.

From atop the creature—on its back or neck or head she couldn't quite be sure, just that her feet steadied themselves on the mountain range of its spine and the fire was trickling far below, far behind—she could see it, the curve of the earth, the horrifying infinitude of the flat-line horizon finally bowing, aching to break, the earth, the whole goddamn universe, confessing itself to be something surmountable, more: combustible. There they were: beyond the quaint fire of her sister's backyard were the blurry paroxysms of other, larger fires, a constellation of them.

She's almost at the tree-house, the edge of its floor just beyond her reach. Charlie is reaching down, offering his hand. It's tempting, both his hand and the lure of naïveté that his tiny body can hoist hers up, but she resists his hand and with it the sure injury the ground would cause them—even more concussing than the impact that same ground made when the creature dropped her back into the yard, back into the awful experiment of this place, from which knowledge of something beyond still does not allow escape—and Vee pulls herself up until she can grip an unsanded edge of lumber, the tree-house's floor. She wedges her foot into the crotch of the tree to boost herself and manages to grab a branch and—her ass and one leg hanging off the edge and threatening to tip her back over like a car caught on a precipice—then scrambles up onto the four-by-four platform that is the entire architectural extent of the tree-house.

And now here she is, huddled on this little Triscuit of an abode, held precariously in this tree. Charlie is beside her, his back against the biggest branch. He's holding the present, clutching it to his chest like a flotation device. His face is lit by the fire, which from up here she can see clearly: it's just over there, a liquid crown on the still-dark yard. No immediate sign of the adults, the stormtrooper. The helicopter is somewhere: she can't see it but she can hear it speedbagging the air nearby.

She looks to Charlie. In such close proximity, he seems shyer now, hiding behind his present.

"Hey," she says. "We made it."

He nods.

"Open your present."

He turns the present around to show her the other side of the box, where the wrapping paper has already been partly ripped away.

"It's okay," she says. "Open it."

He continues pulling at the torn-off paper, flays the box clean in one motion and lets the breeze take the loose crumple of bright paper.

Charlie holds the cardboard box, a repurposed shoebox whose aerodynamic brand has been redacted by thick black Sharpie. A single tab of scotch tape keeps the top of the box from flapping open. Charlie doesn't see the tape and can't pull open the box.

"Here," Vee says. She takes the box, peels off the tape, and hands it back to Charlie. He opens the box. She rolls the bit of tape between her thumb and forefinger.

He pulls the toy from the box, holds it up. Vee shoves the empty box out of the way and it falls to the ground below.

He grips the simple dinosaur with both hands, the thing curved like a single muscle. He holds it out in front of him, moves it through the air as if it's walking or swimming or flying, instantly animating it to life.

She puts her arm around him, gets an over-the-shoulder peek into his world of hermetic play, insulated from the world that burns all around them. It's insulated from her too, to be sure, but just as long as she knows that this world can still exist, can still, even in extremis, discover and protect itself—that's enough.

She squeezes his shoulder. In the distance, she can see the glimmer of the shiny wrapping paper floating out above the flames, being volleyed in the sky by the fire-rippled air, too light itself to ever float down into the flames, just flittering above, until it does, finally, catch in a fit of flame, and suddenly lighter than air, the wrapping paper has its own lonely apotheosis of fire, flies up and away. "Happy birthday, buddy."

"Thanks, Aunt Vee."

He continues to let the dinosaur adventure through an invisible world.

He says, "It's hard to breathe." He gives a sigh that she knows is actually a gentle gasp for air.

"I know, baby. It's the fire. I'm having trouble too."

"Is it getting closer?"

She coughs. "Do you like your present?"

"I like it."

"Does he have a name?"

"Is the fire gonna burn us all up?"

"Here," she says, lifting the bottom of her shirt to his face. "Breathe through the cloth. It'll filter the smoke."

He lets her hold her shirt to his snout. His breath

makes the oval of fabric across his open mouth go concave on inhale, convex on exhale. He plays with his gift.

She hears someone kicking the cardboard box down below them. Then a voice, too angry to be identified: "Here, over here! She's up here!"

Vee pulls Charlie to her, tucks her feet closer, away from the edge of the tree-house. The tips of her Chuck Taylors are only a hand's length from the edge, from giving them away.

A sharp glare of light shines up at them, finds the cracks between the boards, bends the shadows of branches around them.

She pulls Charlie's face to her, to keep him quiet and calm but mostly quiet. He's compliant. More, he melts into her embrace.

A few more lights glare up at them, but she's pretty certain she and Charlie have been untouched by the scanning lights, that the people below, though piqued by the discovery of the fallen box, don't have a visual confirmation.

Charlie begins to squirm. In her anxiety, she has hugged him into her armpit, and now he's struggling to breathe. She lets his head out and he gulps scorched air.

Below, a man shouts, "Step to the edge of the platform with your hands raised!"

Charlie wipes his nose on her shirt and says, "Are they going to kill us?"

"Maybe," Vee says. She hears herself, sees the calm acceptance of doom on the child's face. "They just might."

He nods. "Okay."

"Did you have a good birthday?"

He's holding the toy dinosaur against her leg. "Yeah."

"Colleen!" It's Pam's voice. "Goddamnit, Colleen, are you up there? Do you have my son?"

She feels Charlie spasm to free himself, to be, at the very least, seen by his mother below, but she can't allow that. Not now. She holds him tight.

The eviscerating beat of the helicopter is getting louder and the thing itself soon arrives. It's now above them. She's sure it's there, but she can't see it for the sudden flood of its light.

The pulse of the propeller blades just above them pushes and pulls at their chests. The air goes machine-gun, the light ecstatic.

A fist-size shadow smears the light before them, rising up and falling back down to lodge into the branches just above them. It comes into focus: a metal canister. It's spewing smoke. The smoke absorbs the light, becomes its own kind of darkness, a dense blanket, smothering sight, burning in a way more insidious and noxious than those flames out there.

She can feel Charlie's body convulse in coughs, but the helicopter above blots out all human sound.

She grabs the trunk and pulls herself up, Charlie sliding down her leg into a fetal position at her feet, and she reaches up to grab the canister. It's hot and she flings it down before her skin can register the pain.

Below, white plumes are waved frantically and futilely by arms whose bodies remain obscured in smoke.

Above, the propeller: this is what it must feel like to be held above a blender.

Behind her, Charlie struggles to breathe; and before her, there's the wall of flame slowly closing in, her own modest conflagration. She's high enough again to see beyond it: there, after the middle-distance darkness, there's the rest of it, the other fires, gathering.

She hears her name—the old one—diced by copter blades into a hundred pieces.

On the ground, the smoke is clearing to reveal a proliferation of stormtroopers, two with guns raised, the one still calmly ablaze, more stormtroopers behind them holding back Pam and Geoff and Ryan and Floyd's wife and the rest of the grown-ups, holding them away from the scene, some of the grown-ups cradling kids—there's Celia and Owen and Waylon and even Declan—some of whom have put back on their conical party hats, ready to reclaim the fire and guns and blood, reclaim it all for the festivities: the horror and the fun, all the same.

Her sister's mouth is forming her old name.

She wants to say something. She will say something. She will open her mouth and will say something that will do something, that will vibrate the air more than this helicopter can, that will move the air to beat at the chests below more than this helicopter can, that will peel back skulls with its sheer velocity, that will untangle the horrible causality of this day and all before it, a chain only inevitable from this the dangling end but which started with pure potential, and choice by choice winnowed choices away into this one needle-tip moment, but she will say something, something that will remind Pam, that will carve out a self against the selves she's been given, that's what the thing she'll say will do, and, even at the point when she might notice the stormtrooper still aflame climbing up to the tree-house, she will keep saying that wondrous and terrifying thing that will do a thing, that will do lots of things, that will move beyond this tree, this yard, that will sour all this fruit and soar and see down on the yard and on the city and the whole shorting circuitry of it all, she'll say a thing that will further fuck the circuits, break the numbers, that will collapse all this, that will give the lie to the conceit of spacetime, shrink it back down into a single flicker of light as simple as an old TV blinking out to final dark, if only to remind Pam, remind her of that moment, that moment when she needed something stronger than memory and, and even at that moment, even when Vee might feel the fiery hand of the stormtrooper grip her ankle, she will even then continue saying the thing that will save her, at least for a moment, that will insulate and protect and open a bubble, as simple as a comic-book dialogue bubble, in which she will exist for the moment of the breath-length of her utterance, the bubble she can pull herself into, and pull Charlie into, that bubble, that perfect cavity in the universe that will dilate with her words, inflate with her exhale, that will cushion her and Charlie from the saw-toothed world for as long as she can say it, this thing that she will say, that will remind her sister of a moment Pam unmoored herself from memory, the two of them did, feeling the chalky shards of chemical amnesia scrape down their throats without water, and she will continue saying this thing even as the stormtrooper's grip on her ankle might undo her bearings on the structure that she built with her two hands, those hands hopeful that she was building something permanent, a permanent place in this home, this structure that will, even when the stormtrooper's grip might become too much, when it just might exert a poundage of pressure upon her person that will feel like the Earth and all its awful gravity concentrated on one linchpin-point of her body, just might pull her body into that gravity, even then she will keep saying the thing, will keep inflating that bubble, dilating that cavity in which she can exist for the single length of a breath, an exhalation manipulated, knotted and squeezed into language, her language, her breath with her tongue upon the stops, and as long as she can maintain the momentum of the thing that she will say, then that moment, that bubble, will last, will float against the sucking current of the fire-distorted wind, even as her body will be pulled into the vacuum of something so fundamental as gravity that it exists *a priori*, so unquestioned and self-sustained that even she can't rage against its influence, even as that influence means a dead-fall toward family, toward her sister for whom she will be recalling the moment after the pill, when they shared a brief kid-like giggle of anticipation, anticipation of surrender, her sister for whom she built this thing, this tree-house, this thing at which she will, when she falls, stare up at, that sad structure, that thing slipping away from her as she will fall away from it, her eyes up, the tree-house itself looking like it is the one falling away from her, not her from it, freefalling, as if falling were free, free of the realities that prove impervious to everything, that exert themselves and press themselves upon one awful hope, even then she will say something, she will she will she will say something, something that will remind Pam of that moment, that moment years ago when, after Dad died, Pam asked her for something, something stronger than memory, and, after they swallowed the halves of the pill without water, Vee, before she was Vee, looked down at her legs, at her arms, now beyond her control, her self removed: a body apart, when Pam reached out, hand weak against the pill's gravity, said she just wanted to touch her, before they both lost feeling.

She opens her mouth to speak.

About the author

Kevin Allardice's first novel, *Any Resemblance to Actual Persons*, was longlisted for the Flaherty-Dunnan First Novel Prize. He was born in Oakland, California, and was a Henry Hoyns fellow in fiction at the University of Virginia, where he received his MFA in 2010. His short stories, winner of the of the Donald Barthelme Prize and twice nominated for a Pushcart Prize, have appeared in *The Santa Monica Review, The Florida Review, Gulf Coast,The North American Review*, and elsewhere. He lives in Berkeley, California.

CPSIA information can be obtained
at www.ICGtesting.com
Printed in the USA
BVOW04s1610250417
482248BV00008B/16/P